FLOSSIE TE
FUR

Flossie Teacake's Fur Coat

HUNTER DAVIES

Illustrated by

Laurence Hutchins

Young Lions

For Flora,
My Own Little Flossie . . .

First published in Great Britain 1982
by The Bodley Head Ltd
First published in Young Lions 1984
Sixth impression May 1988

Young Lions is an imprint of
the Children's Division, part of
the Collins Publishing Group,
8 Grafton Street, London W1X 3LA

Printed and bound in Great Britain by
William Collins Sons & Co. Ltd, Glasgow

CONTENTS

1

Introducing Flossie

Flossie Teacake was sitting at the tea table. It was liver, which she hated, and onions, which looked yucky, and green salad, ugh, which she always refused to touch.

"It's not fair," said Flossie. "You always make things *they* like but never make things I like."

"Oh, shut up, Flossie," said her big sister Bella.

"Why should I?" said Flossie. "I'm not a shop."

Flossie thought this was a pretty smart reply, but the others were too busy eating to notice, treating Flossie as if she wasn't there.

Her big brother Fergus and her big sister Isabella, known as Bella, were both eating so quickly and so furiously that Flossie imagined they were in some sort of race.

"You should be on TV, you two," said Flossie.

"In one of those stupid competitions. It's a Blow-Out. That would be a good name for a stupid competition, as you're both so stupid . . ."

She expected some sort of reaction this time, if only a push in the ribs, just to prove she was *there*, at the tea table with her family, but they still ignored her. At the same time as Fergus and Bella were filling themselves full of food, watching each other to make sure no one got thirds before they'd finished their seconds, they were also talking at the top of their voices. Yatter, yatter, yatter.

"I only got a B in that essay, Mum," said Bella. "I really should have got a much better mark because . . ."

"He's been dropped from the team, Mum," said Fergus. "They haven't a chance now, yet last week he was their best player . . ."

Bella, as usual, was talking about her school work, which was very boring for Flossie because Bella was at Big School. Fergus was going on about his favourite football team which again was very boring for Flossie. She hated football.

"Won't you try some of that nice salad, Flossie?" said Mother. "There's a good girl."

"How can salad be nice," said Flossie. "All salad is horrid."

"Don't be so cheeky," said Fergus. "Anyway, I want it all."

"Don't be a pig," said Bella. "I haven't had any yet."

Flossie didn't really mind having to sit at the tea table while her brother and sister tucked into their disgusting food. She had her food to come. It was chocolate cake for pudding. Yum, yum. Flossie was willing to put up with almost anything, if there was pudding at the end of it.

It was a family rule that everyone had to sit down at the table together and everyone had to sit there till the end. There was no coming and going. No reading at the table. And most important of all, no carrying plates around. Certainly not carrying plates to the television.

Flossie's mother, however, did not mind if you didn't like things. The rule was that if you didn't want certain things, then you didn't take them. Flossie's mother hated people who took things, and *then* left them.

Flossie was very fond of cucumber, but cucumber

wasn't on today. Once, when she was very little, so her mother told her, she had lived on nothing but cucumber for a whole week. She got very thin and her mother got very, very worried but then Flossie changed to biscuits and lived on them instead.

"Aren't there any biscuits, Mum?" asked Flossie, putting on her polite voice. "I could live on biscuits. There's a lot of iron in biscuits, you know."

"What rubbish," said Bella.

"You think *you* know everything," said Flossie. "Those ginger biscuits. They're full of iron. That's why they're brown."

"You know you're not allowed biscuits, dear," said Mother. "Not during the week."

Flossie wasn't fat. She was just a little bit plump. Mother always tried to keep an eye on her diet to make sure she didn't eat *too* many sweet things. What Flossie wanted most in this world was to be tall and thin, just like her big sister Bella.

They were still yattering away. Bella was now talking about an important examination which might or might not get her into University. Flossie hoped very much she passed it and got to University and left home because Flossie had been promised her room. There was nothing in the whole world that Flossie wanted more than to have Bella's room.

There were in fact *lots* of things in this big wide world which Flossie wanted very much. Bella's room—and being tall and thin—just happened to be two of them.

"He shouldn't have been dropped," said Fergus, returning to the subject of football once again.

"Didn't it hurt his head?" asked Flossie. Fergus took no notice of Flossie. He got up and went to the fridge to pour himself some more orange juice.

"Sit down, Fergus," said his mother. "You know you're not allowed to get up during tea. You should have made sure you had enough to drink before you sat down."

Flossie liked to hear her big brother and her big sister being told off. It seemed to her she was *always* the one being told off.

"When he was dropped," said Flossie, "didn't it hurt the footballer's head?"

"Ha, ha, very funny," said Fergus.

"Yes, I thought so," said Flossie.

"You can go back to sleep now," said Fergus to Flossie. "Specky Four Eyes . . ."

"That's a horrid thing to say, Fergus," said her mother, very cross. "I've told you about that before."

"Sorry, Flossie," said Fergus. "Sor-ree."

Flossie often did think of good jokes, funny things to say, interesting things to say, but at tea-time the others never gave her a chance. It *wasn't* fair. She wished her mother would hurry up and cut the cake.

It was only in the last few months that Flossie had been forced to wear spectacles. She was suffering from something called astigmatism. All it meant was that she had a very, very slight squint in one eye.

Her mother had promised Flossie that she would *not* have to wear spectacles for ever. If she was a good girl and wore them till she was fourteen, then her eyes would be perfect, because they would have grown and changed by then, and she would never have to wear spectacles, ever again. Oh, if only she could be fourteen now.

Flossie was nine years old. Her birthday was on October 31, Hallowe'en. Every year it was on Hallowe'en. (That was one of Flossie's jokes.) She was very proud, as it made her seem rather special.

She would have hated to have been born on April Fool's Day. And she would not have liked to have been born on Christmas Day. Bella and Fergus, being mean, would then have cheated and only given her one present every Christmas Day, not two.

Bella was eighteen years old. She was grown up, really, as far as Flossie was concerned. Fergus was sixteen years old. He was just stupid and silly, like all boys. As far as Flossie was concerned.

Flossie's full name was Flora MacDonald MacDougal MacSporran Teacake. Bella's full name was Isabella Iona Glasgow Edinburgh Teacake. Fergus was Fergus Duncan Dougal Hector Teacake. They had all been given Scottish names because their father had been born in Scotland and he was very proud of being Scottish. It was a shame he had such a silly surname as Teacake. He had thought of changing his surname by deed poll, but his mother—Flossie's grandmother—would simply not hear of it. Teacake had been good enough for Teacakes for centuries. Every Teacake had been called Teacake. So that was that.

Flossie *used* to like being called Flossie, when she was little, but now she had decided it was babyish, or it sounded like a doll, or perhaps a kitten. But it was too late now.

She had changed her name the other week to Karen, but nobody had noticed and had carried on calling her Flossie. Then she told everyone she was to be called Cindy, but everyone had still persisted in addressing her as Flossie. For one whole weekend she was Tracy, and wrote Tracy all over her new books, but her mother got very cross and made her rub it out. The books had been presents from her grandmother. Her grandmother hated the name Tracy. Flossie had considered calling herself Sheena, but she didn't know how to spell it.

There would be no problem when she was grown up, when she had become a teenager like Bella. She would then call herself Floz. She'd already decided that. She would allow nobody to call her such a babyish name as Flossie, ever again. When you are grown up, so Flossie thought, people *have* to take notice of you.

There was a knock at the front door and Flossie jumped up. She had just started to eat her cake but she liked going to the front door and very often it was for her. Two girls from her class lived in her street, and they usually came to call for her to play after they'd had their tea.

"I'll go," said Bella, pushing Flossie out of the way. "It will be for me."

"Horrible," said Flossie.

"You're the horrible one," said Bella, making a face at Flossie, but by the time Bella had got into the hall and was opening the door, she was all smiles and jokes. Ha ha, ho ho.

Flossie could hear Bella laughing with her friends, then there was a lot of banging and crashing, and more laughs and noise, as they all went up the stairs to Bella's room.

Bella always had huge gangs of friends coming to see her, teenage boys and girls, all wearing strange clothes and strange hair and strange make-up. They had such good times. It wasn't fair.

Then they all came back downstairs again, still laughing and shouting. Flossie wanted to go and see them, to hide behind the front door, and just catch a little sight of them, not get in the way, not annoy Bella. Bella didn't like Flossie spying on her and her friends.

"I'm just going out, Mum," said Bella, putting her head round the living-room door. "O.K.?"

"If you say so, dear," said Mother. "But what about your essay?"

"Oh, Mum, it's Friday night. I'll do that tomorrow."

"If you say so, dear," said Mother. "But don't be late."

"We'll probably end up at the pub," said Bella. "I won't be later than eleven o'clock. Promise."

And with that, Bella had gone, in a flurry of silks and satins, beads and bangles.

Flossie had noticed that in just the few minutes she had spent upstairs, Bella had managed to throw on some even more strange clothes. And she definitely had eye-shadow on. Flossie had seen that straight away. It wasn't fair. And those jangling ear-rings. They were so long and jangly they almost came down to the floor. Flossie hoped she tripped and fell over them.

Flossie had *once* been allowed make-up. It had been for her birthday party, on Hallowe'en, and she had been dressed as a witch. She tried to keep some of it on for the next day, to go to school, to let her friends see, but her mother had noticed and made her wipe all of it off. It wasn't fair.

When she was eighteen, the first thing she would do would be to dye her hair pink. Flossie considered her hair to be so boring anyway, just sort of thin and straggling. The only thing you could do with it was dye it.

Bella's hair had already been every colour of the rainbow, plus some shades you never see in rainbows, not even the rainbows on the tops of boxes of paints. It had once turned out green with yellow streaks, but that had been a mistake. It should have been yellow, with green streaks.

Flossie stood in the hall on her own. There was a strong whiff of perfume which lingered on long after Bella and her friends had departed.

"What about your piano practice?" said Mother.

"Oh God, do I have to?" said Flossie, throwing herself on a cushion.

"Don't say 'Oh God'. Your grandmother doesn't like it."

"She's not here, stupid," said Flossie. "She's in

Scotland, stupid."

Mother just smiled. Normally, she might have told Flossie off, for being so rude, but she realized Flossie was in one of her moods.

"I hate the piano. I'm giving it up."

"What about those thank-you letters? Have you written them yet, Flossie?"

"Yes, I have," said Flossie, which was a lie. "Then I threw them all in the dustbin."

"How about some sticking? You haven't done any sticking for such a long time."

"That's 'cos it's stupid. And drawing's stupid. Everybody's stupid in this house. And horrible to me."

Flossie did some head-stands on the cushions, banging her feet loudly on the floor as she came down, too loudly, just to show she was annoyed. She swept a few felt pens off the table, and then did some cart-wheels right across the room, landing very heavily each time. Being ever so slightly plump, even when Flossie landed lightly, she still made quite a bit of noise.

Mother was smiling as she stood in the kitchen, loading up the dish-washer. Fergus announced that he was going out to play snooker at someone's house. He wouldn't be late either. Not more than ten o'clock.

Ten o'clock! Flossie's bedtime was eight o'clock, even on a Friday night with no school tomorrow. Fair, it was not.

She gave a quick kick at Fido, their large and dopey retriever, who was lying half asleep in front of the television. Fido looked at the screen, wondering if someone had jumped out of "It's a Knock-Out" and hit him by mistake, then he realized it had been Flossie. It wasn't a very hard kick, not that Fido would have minded. He loved all the Teacakes, especially Flossie Teacake.

Having done all that, Flossie felt much better. She went to the piano and did half an hour's very good practice. Mother was very pleased. Then Flossie went to bed.

"I'll put myself to bed, thank you," said Flossie, defiantly, just to show she didn't care.

"There's a good girl. Daddy will tuck you up when we come to bed."

Dad wasn't home yet, Friday was his late night. But no matter how late he was, he always went into

Flossie's bedroom, last thing at night, and tucked her up, just to make sure she was all right and comfy humphry.

Flossie's bedroom was at the top of the house, beside Bella's and Fergus's, but it was the smallest of the three. It was very neat and tidy, with all her school photographs on the wall, pinned in order, from the nursery school right up to the Second Year Juniors, which was the class she was now in.

There were some satin picture postcards of dolls, which Dad had sent her, and some little glass animals, set out in order of size on a shelf. On her table, beautifully arranged, were her best felt pens, not the second best set which were kept downstairs.

She looked around her room, at all her possessions, so well ordered and arranged, and gave a long, low sigh.

"I hate my room. It's not fair."

She stood at the top of the stairs and listened. She heard Fergus go out, which wasn't hard, the whole world could hear Fergus when he was going out.

Her mother was still in the kitchen, getting a meal ready for Dad.

Very slowly, Flossie tiptoed to the door of Bella's room and listened carefully. Bella had so many friends always coming and going that there might still be one of them inside. She listened for a long time, but the room seemed empty.

Bella had lots of notices on the outside of her door saying, "Keep Out, Guard Dogs, Dangerous, No Admittance and This Means You, Flossie." Flossie didn't even bother to read them. She knew them by heart.

No one was allowed in Bella's room, least of all Flossie. Even Mother had given up trying to get in to clean it and just left it as it was. If Bella wanted it that way, then it was her concern.

Flossie very carefully tried to push the door open, but it seemed to be stuck. Perhaps there was a lock on it. That would be really a rotten trick. Trust Bella. Always horrible. Imagine putting on a lock and key, just to stop your little sister. Really horrible.

Flossie managed to get it a few inches open, and could then see it wasn't locked after all, so she decided to give it an extra push.

Flossie landed in the room with a crash and a hat stand fell just in front of her. It narrowly missed her head. It had obviously been a trap, to catch any intruders trying to get into Bella's room.

Flossie often heard loud noises in Bella's room late at night, usually from Bella. She must sometimes hit herself with her own traps, having forgotten she had set them. Serve her right. Rotten thing.

Flossie stood up and looked around. She hadn't been into Bella's room for months and months and months and months. It was like an Aladdin's cave. Every surface was a mass of cushions and clothes, pillows and rugs. Bella had even managed to hang things from the ceiling with nails. Wait till Dad saw those.

Flossie gave a little jump, frightened by the sight of some sheep's skulls in a corner, surrounded by what looked like the heads of real people. She thought about leaving at once.

Very slowly, she realized that they were models, the heads of dummies you see in shop windows. It was all so gloomy. The rugs and clothing covered the window as well as all the walls and ceiling.

One corner was full of empty bottles and jars and in another there were old lamps and "Road Up" signs. Flossie could also see lots of records and posters and pages cut out of colour magazines.

The room was littered with old clothes, as if Bella was about to open a shop. They lay in piles everywhere, all incredibly dirty, dusty and messy. That was what Flossie liked best of all. There was no order, no neatness, anywhere in the whole of the room.

"Oh, if only I could have a room like this," thought Flossie to herself. "I'd love to wear all these funny clothes."

Still listening very carefully, she climbed over the piles and heaps and found Bella's make-up table, which was not a table but a strip of red silk material, laid out on the carpet in a corner.

Then she noticed Bella's necklaces and ear-rings and jewellery, hanging from the fingers and arms of a life-sized statue, just above her head. Flossie didn't dare touch anything, for fear of leaving marks and being found out. She just stared and stared.

Beside the statue was a large wooden coat stand,

an old-fashioned one, with curly corners, painted shocking pink. It was covered in about ten of Bella's old coats. On top was a fur coat which Flossie had never seen before.

Bella spent a lot of time at jumble sales, buying old clothes, all for pennies, or so she told Flossie, though she had to fight for them.

Flossie always tried to be around when Bella came home, just to see her latest purchases. She recognized quite a few things, but she had never seen this fur coat, never in her life before.

The fur coat was very dark and shiny, not quite black, but there were many black streaks in it. It looked enormous, as if it had once belonged to a bear, but a very rich, prosperous, millionaire bear.

Flossie stared at it for a long time. She seemed to be able to see strange shapes in its silky, shiny surface. As she moved her head, looking at it from all angles, different faces seemed to be staring out at her. Or was she imagining it?

She wondered if she could possibly try it on. Could she dare? Would Bella ever find out?

"Bella will be in the pub by now," thought Flossie to herself. "She'll be laughing and joking with all her friends. No one knows I'm in her bedroom."

Flossie went over to the bedroom door and listened down the stairs, just in case. All she could hear was a faint sniffing. It sounded like Fergus unable to find a handkerchief but it must be Fido. He wasn't allowed upstairs. She could hear her own heart beating very loudly.

She went back inside Bella's room, stepping carefully over all the piles, and began stroking the fur coat. It couldn't possibly do any harm, just *stroking* a coat. She was probably doing it good.

"Bella might be grateful to me," thought Flossie. "Keeping the hair in order, making it all shiny. Perhaps she might pay me a penny a week to come and look after her coat.

"No, of course she won't. Bella is always horrid to me. She won't let me touch *any* of her things. Horrible."

There was now complete silence from down below. Even Fido must have got fed up and gone for another sleep.

"Coats are meant for wearing, aren't they," said Flossie to herself. "It will do it good to be worn. Just for a few moments. It's probably lonely, hanging up here all the time, doing nothing, going nowhere."

Very carefully, she took down the coat. It turned out not to be as heavy as it appeared, but even so, it was terribly big, far too big for Flossie. Just by looking at it, she could see it would come right down to the floor. All the same, she decided to try it on. Just once. Very quickly. No one would ever know.

"Oh, I'd love a coat like this," thought Flossie, snuggling deep inside the fur.

She pulled the collar up so that only the tiny tip of her nose was peeping out. There was a long mirror on one wall, a broken one, which Bella had found in a builder's skip. Flossie stepped carefully across to it and admired her reflection.

"Will I ever be old enough to wear a coat like this?"

There was a slight noise on the stairs and she stopped, listened, but it was just the house creaking.

She closed her eyes, gave three turns, then another, just for luck, wishing with all her might that she could be eighteen years old, this very minute, and

not a boring nine-year-old with specs and a fat tummy and bossed around by everyone and told to eat green salad.

She stood with her eyes closed, feeling the coat around her, so big it was almost like a tent. As she felt it, she realized there were three buttons down the front she hadn't noticed before. Very slowly, she began to button them up, starting from the bottom. As she did up the top button, something strange seemed to happen to her. It was as if her body was growing inside the coat, as if some sort of magic was at work.

She opened her eyes and looked in the mirror and saw herself emerging like a butterfly. (Or was it a chrysalis? Miss Button had been doing that in class this morning, but Flossie had forgotten the words.)

The most astonishing transformation had taken place. Flossie *was* now eighteen years old. She had jumped forward in time, almost ten years. She was still herself, but herself as a teenager.

Very, very carefully, she examined herself in the mirror. She recognized herself, but all the same, she had to feel her hair just to see if it was real. It was. She wet her fingers and licked it, fearing it might be candyfloss. The pink colour stayed in. She must have used a very good dye. And the mascara under her eyes. That was real as well.

Then she noticed the biggest difference of all. She was *not* wearing spectacles. Her mother was right. She had given them up. Her eyes were perfect, now that she was eighteen. No one could ever tease her about having a squint, ever again.

The fur coat, she now realized, fitted her perfectly. Not too long. Not too short. She undid the bottom two buttons, just enough to let her see how tall and thin she was, as tall and thin and grown up as Bella.

She came down the stairs slowly, not wishing to shock anyone. She caught sight of herself in the landing mirror, and saw that she did look every inch an eighteen-year-old. She fastened all the buttons tightly again, and snuggled inside. She did not want to take her fur coat off. If she did, well, she didn't know what might happen . . .

2

Flossie Goes to the Pub

"Just off to the pub," Floz heard herself gaily shout as she came downstairs. She had decided the moment she walked out of Bella's room that now she was grown up, she would be called Floz. On the outside at least, she was no longer that plump little nine-year-old called Flossie.

"Oh, hello," said her mother, coming out of the living room. "I thought everyone had gone."

Despite the transformation, Floz had expected her mother to recognize her. After all, she was still her daughter, still the same girl underneath. But her mother obviously thought she was another of Bella's friends. They were always wandering round the house.

"Did you notice if Flossie was asleep?" asked her mother.

"Yeh, sound asleep," said Floz, pulling her fur coat tightly around herself. "When I was her age, I used to be sound asleep at this time of night."

"Oh, that's good," said her mother. "She was a bit bad-tempered when she went upstairs. I knew she would soon get over it. She gets so upset by Bella going out and having a good time."

"Yes, I can quite understand it," said Floz.

As Floz walked down the hall to the front door, the door opened and in walked her father. He too smiled, but stared right through her, showing no signs of recognition.

Fido came bounding out to meet Mr Teacake, then he jumped all over Floz. She tried very hard to push him off, worried that he might dirty or even tear her fur coat.

"Oh, you've made a hit," said Father. "He doesn't usually go for strangers. Not that you're a stranger, of course. I have seen you around the house before, haven't I . . . ?"

"Oh, yes, Mr Teacake, many times."

"By the way, what's your name? I seem to have forgotten it . . ."

"Eh, Floz. Yes, Floz. That's it. I'd better hurry. I

want to catch them up. They'll be in the pub by now. Cheerio . . ."

Mr and Mrs Teacake exchanged quick glances, thinking what a strange girl. All the same, there was something familiar about her, almost as if they had seen her somewhere before . . .

Floz hurried through the front door, then nearly fell over going down the path. Her stiletto heels were terribly high. She hadn't quite got used to them. She hoped no one was watching her, back in the house.

She turned round and saw a little soft, wet, furry nose appearing round the doorway, watching her carefully, then the door was closed, very firmly. Only Fido had realized what had happened and who she really was.

"Now, which pub should I go to?"

There was the Cat and Fiddle on the High Street and the Dog and Duck near the park. She knew that Bella and her friends went to both of these. Naturally, she had never been to either in her life before.

"But I'm eighteen now," said Floz to herself. "Of course I am. I must be. Look how tall I am." She

hugged her lovely fur coat to herself and set off in the direction of the Cat and Fiddle.

As she walked along, she practised looking over hedges and walls into other people's front doors and front windows. She had never been able to see so much before. It really was very useful, being five feet six inches tall instead of just four feet four inches high.

"This is much better than being on stilts," thought Floz. "Clowns on stilts always look so silly. You can always see their stiff legs."

One or two people smiled at her, but she didn't want to smile back, just in case she smudged her lipstick, or ruined her mascara, or started her ear-rings jangling. If they got going, they might go round and round like the Big Wheel at the Fair, then she would feel very dizzy indeed.

"I mustn't giggle either," thought Floz. "If I giggle too much, I might fall off my high heels."

So Flossie—sorry, Floz—walked very carefully down the middle of the pavement, looking to neither left nor right.

She had once, a very long time ago when she was nine, been in a pub in the country with her grandmother, but she couldn't really remember it. Anyway, it was only in the pub's garden, though she had boasted at school she had been in a real pub. She had certainly never been inside a town pub.

She got to the Cat and Fiddle and saw two glass doors. She pressed her nose against the first one which said "Public Bar". That seemed very silly. If it was Public, why did they keep it closed? She deliberately made a funny face, as she pressed her nose against the glass. She always did this, when she pressed her nose against any sort of window.

She went to the other door and this one was marked "Private Saloon". That looked more like it. Now she was eighteen, she could go anywhere, do anything. "Private" obviously referred to silly little children of nine years old. No one wanted them in pubs, did they. Certainly not.

Floz opened the glass door of the pub and went inside. It turned out to be a very big room with red seats, a red carpet and a big red flashing box playing pop music which nobody seemed to be listening to.

Floz could see lots of little tables, with a few

people sitting at them, but hardly any of the people seemed to be talking to each other.

When she had seen pubs on television, they were always full of people laughing and talking, or standing up holding glasses in their hands and singing as if they were in some sort of competition. There was always a very pretty lady with blonde hair who gave out the drinks. All she could see in this pub, if it really was a pub, was a very old man in a cardigan who was wiping the table with a very old tea towel, the sort her mother gave Fergus to clean his bike with.

She was beginning to think it wasn't a pub, and that she had walked into some sort of school for old people.

"Perhaps the old man has been naughty," thought Floz, "and he's wiping the tables as a punishment."

Then she noticed in one corner, at a large table, Bella and her friends, sitting all together. One of the boys with Bella, a boy she recognized, gave her a wave, beckoning her to come over.

Floz looked around, just to check he wasn't waving at someone else, or perhaps putting his hand up, wanting Miss to let him leave the classroom. But no. There was no one else around. So she went across and sat down with them.

"Hi," said Martin. Floz knew he was called Martin because he was Bella's boyfriend and had been to her house many times. *One* of Bella's boyfriends. She had so many.

Bella was looking at Floz with a funny expression on her face. Floz worried about what she might say. Would she recognize her? What if she realized what had happened?

"That's a nice coat," said Bella. "I used to have one like that. Got it at a jumble. But it didn't suit me. You look great in it."

"Thanks," said Floz, giving a big smile.

"Didn't I see you at the school play last night?" asked Martin.

"I dunno," said Floz. "How do I know."

Her mother was always trying to stop her saying "I dunno" or even worse, "How do I know." But her mother wasn't here to stop her. When you're in a pub, you can say what you like. That's what pubs are for, thought Floz.

"Seen you somewhere anyway," said Martin. "What would you like to drink then?"

"Hmm," said Floz, thinking hard. She couldn't decide. Her favourite drink was really Ribena, but this didn't look like a place that served Ribena, or ice cream.

"I'll have a Coke, please," she said.

"How do you want it," asked Martin. "With rum, whisky, gin?"

"With a straw," replied Floz.

They all started laughing. Martin said what a good idea, really great, wish he'd thought of that.

"It will make the drinks last longer," said Martin.

When they saw Floz drinking with a straw, they told Martin to bring back straws for them. Very soon, all of them were drinking their drinks with straws.

At the next table, another group decided they too would have straws. Floz watched the old man in the cardigan. He seemed to be the only one who didn't think it was funny.

Floz was very pleased that they all thought she was so amusing and original, but very soon, they got talking about examinations, a subject Floz had always found very boring, so she got up and had a walk round the pub. She wanted to see what it really looked like.

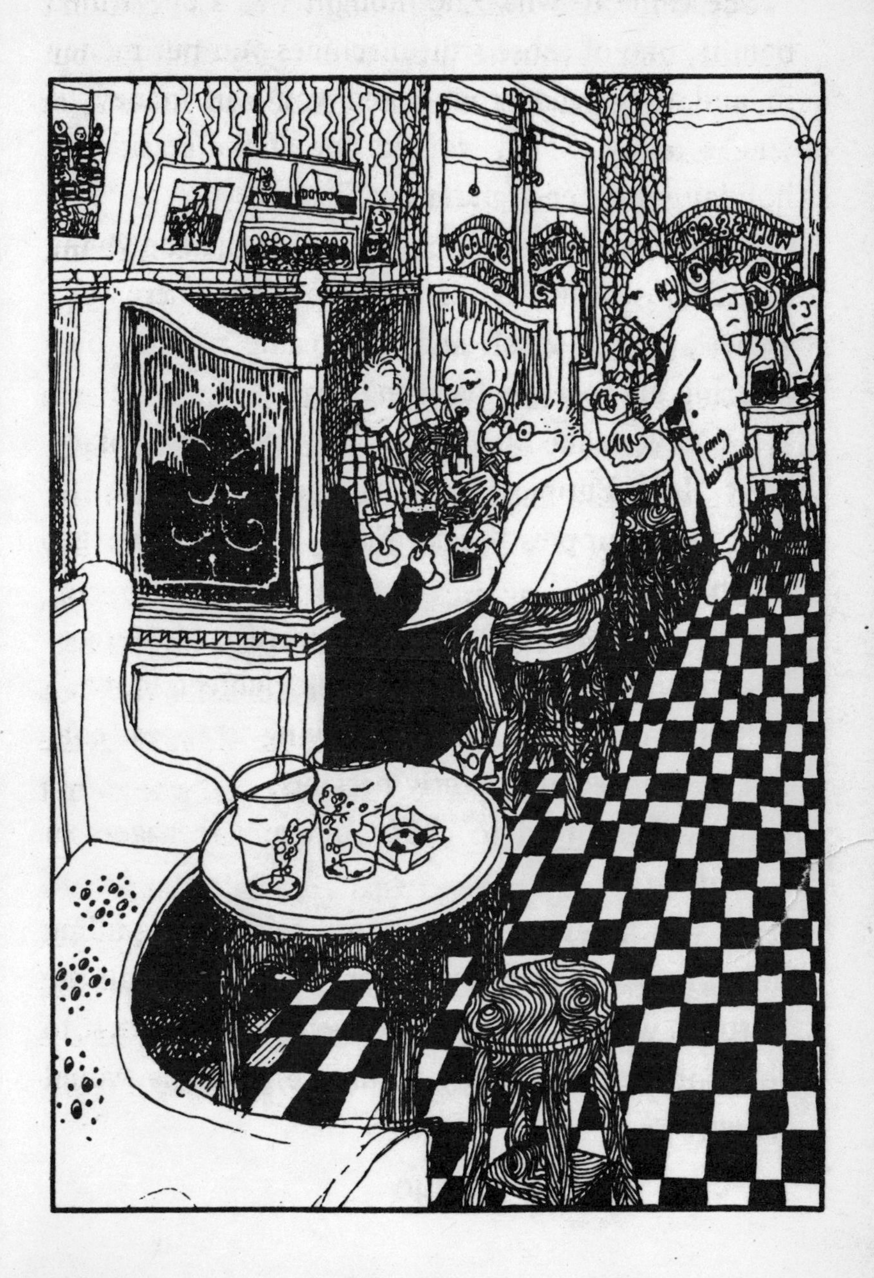

She came to what she thought was a one-armed bandit, one of those fruit machines you put money in and they whirl round and you win money, if you're lucky. She'd worked one at the seaside on holiday with her grandfather.

Floz leaned over the counter and pushed down the handle, just to find out if it was working. There was a swoosh and a swish and beer came rushing out, pouring all over the barman's legs.

"You've soaked my shoes," he said, very crossly. "My Hush Puppies. Look at them."

"Slush Puppies," said Floz. "Now you've got Slush Puppies."

"How old are you?" asked the barman, looking at her suspiciously. "You don't look eighteen to me."

"Oh, very old," said Floz, trying to appear confident, but feeling slightly nervous.

"I've been told to chuck out any teenagers of seventeen."

"I was seventeen *years* ago," said Floz, pulling her fur coat tightly round her, making sure all the buttons were done up. She went quickly back to the corner, as quickly as her high heels would allow.

Bella was still talking about exams, saying she hadn't done enough work, not with A-levels coming up. She couldn't get much done anyway, not in her house. Her little fat sister was such a pest, getting in the way, making a noise all the time.

"She's not fat," said Floz.

"How do you know?" said Bella. "I didn't know you'd ever met her."

"Oh, I've seen her around," said Floz.

"She must be fat," said Martin. "If you've seen her a-round. Get it?" Floz laughed. She liked those sort of jokes. She stretched out her legs, admiring how long and thin they were.

"I didn't know you lived in this area?" said Bella to Floz, ignoring Martin.

"Sometimes I do," said Floz. "Sometimes I don't."

"Which school are you at?" asked Bella.

"Don't be so nosy, Bella," said Martin.

"Second Year Juniors," said Floz. "Miss Button's class."

Once more, they all laughed. Only Bella seemed worried about Floz, staring at her carefully, trying to work out something, as if wondering where exactly they'd met before.

"What's your name?" said Bella.

"What's your number?" said Martin, before Floz could reply.

"Cucumber," said Floz, very quickly.

"What's your station?" said Martin.

"Eggs and Bacon," said Floz.

"Oh, don't be so silly," said Bella. "You're not in Primary School now."

"O.K., you can call me Floz," said Floz. "That's my name now."

"You mean you change it all the time?" said Martin.

"Oh, yes," said Floz. "Last week I was Cindy. Then I used to be Tracy."

They all started laughing once again, slapping Floz on the back. Only Bella looked slightly puzzled, as if she were remembering something. One of the boys insisted on buying Floz another drink, and before she could stop him, he had come back with half a pint of beer. The glass seemed to be full of bits and pieces floating around. Floz looked at it for a long time. She had never tasted beer before. She had once had a sip of her father's sherry, and that was yucky, and her grandmother had once let her taste a glass of something called egg flip, and that was even yuckier.

"It's real beer," said the boy.

"Oh," said Floz. "I usually drink pretend beer."

The boy laughed, and then he started talking with Martin and the other boys about different sorts of beers and different sorts of pubs. It was a change from talking about exams, but the evening did seem to be going on for an awful long time. Floz had thought that teenagers did more exciting things than this. All the same, she was sitting in a real pub with real teenagers drinking real beer, not being bossed around by anyone.

While they were talking, she at last took a quick sip. It was horrible, even worse than she had imagined. She got up, holding her glass, deciding she would take another walk.

In a corner, a man was playing a machine which she hadn't noticed before. There were lights flashing and buzzers buzzing and lots of other electronic noises. It was a Space Invader. Floz was absolutely delighted. She'd once seen one in a motorway café, but of course she hadn't been allowed to play it. They'd only stopped for petrol. The Teacakes do not believe in going inside motorway cafés.

"Oh, brilliant," said Floz, putting her glass of beer on top of the machine. "After you, please."

"Don't put that there," said the man.

"It's a present for you," said Floz. "I just bought it for you."

"Cheers," said the man, without even looking round.

"Hip, hip, hooray," said Floz.

The man soon stopped, took a drink of the beer which Floz had given him, and let her take over the machine, which was very kind of him, even explaining to her how to work it.

Floz undid the bottom button of her fur coat, just to give herself more freedom of movement, so she could use both arms at the same time.

"This is really great," said Floz, getting all excited, working the controls and shouting and shrieking. She undid the next button.

"You're doing very well," said the man. "But I'd

take your coat off, if I were you."

Floz had her fingers on the top button when she felt a strange sensation in her tummy. She stopped at once.

"I think I'll just sit down now," she said. Had it been something to do with that top button? Or had it been that mouthful of revolting beer which made her feel so funny? Floz didn't want to take any chances. She went back and sat down with her new friends.

"Time, ladies and gentlemen, please," shouted the Cardigan Man. He happened to be standing near Floz and she got quite a fright.

"Sorry," said Floz to the Cardigan Man. "I don't know the time."

"What are you talking about?" said the Cardigan Man.

"I haven't got a watch," said Floz. "I did have a Mickey Mouse one, with pretend hands, but it's broken . . ."

"Don't be so cheeky," said the Cardigan Man. "Come on, let's have you. Everyone out."

"Why don't we all go back to my place," said Martin. "You can all have coffee. You can come as well, Floz."

"Sorry, Martin," said Floz. "I have to be home by eleven. That's when my Daddy comes upstairs and tucks me in," she said.

They all laughed so much that Floz thought the Cardigan Man might be very angry this time.

She waved them quickly goodbye at the doorway of the pub, then ran off as fast as she could on her high heels for home. She realized it was absolutely vital to be back home and in bed before anyone found out.

Only Bella and Fergus were officially allowed to use the secret method of getting into their house, not little Flossie. Little Flossie couldn't do it anyway.

It meant stretching high and putting your arm through the letter box, then twisting and turning so you could unlock the door from the inside. Flossie's hand was too small to manage such a trick, but Floz, being so tall and thin and ever so grown up, she managed to do it quite easily.

She took her stilettos off as soon as she got inside, but immediately Fido dashed into the hall to greet her, sniffing and licking her legs. She was scared everyone would come into the hall to see who it was, but nothing happened. She gave Fido a hug, then gently pushed him away, giving him a big wave, and raced upstairs. She went straight into Bella's bedroom and began to take off the fur coat.

She undid the buttons, starting from the bottom, and as she reached the top and final button, her body seemed suddenly to shrink. It all happened so quickly. One instant she was a tall eighteen-year-old. The next, she was little Flossie again, only nine. The fur coat was now on her shoulders, overwhelming her, feeling very heavy and enormous. It almost fell off of its own accord. Flossie picked it up and hung it carefully on the coat stand.

Then Flossie ran into her own little bedroom, put on her little pyjamas and got under the blankets. A few minutes later, her father came up the stairs. Flossie closed her eyes very tightly.

"Ah, she's asleep," said her father, but very softly, not wanting to waken Flossie. "Good girl. I wonder where that Bella is, out in the pub at this time of night. Good job we still have one little girl in the family.

"Oh, what's this on the floor. A straw, it looks like. Now where did that come from? Smells funny as well."

He bent down, tucked in all the blankets, and gave Flossie a kiss.

"Goodnight, Flossie," said her father. "Sleep well. And don't grow up too quickly . . ."

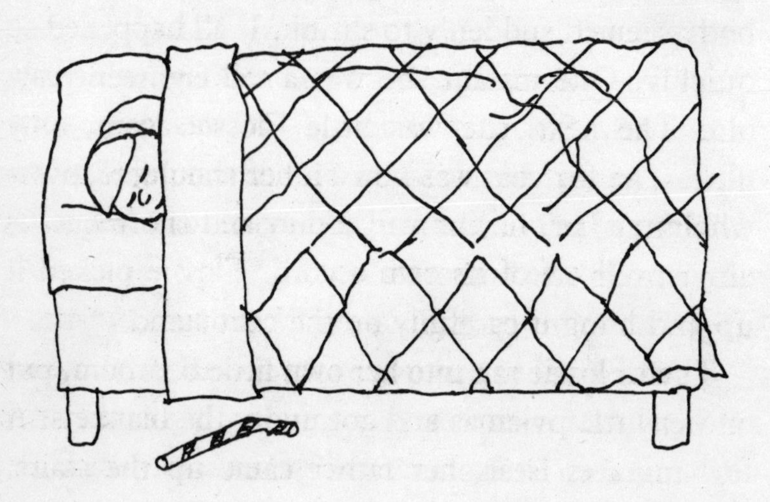

3

Flossie Becomes a Waitress

It was Saturday morning and Flossie Teacake was the only one of the Teacakes up and out of bed and downstairs.

Flossie was making her own breakfast, which she did every Saturday morning. It was only corn-flakes, so that hadn't taken a lot of making. She was allowed to put on the grill and make toast but today she couldn't be bothered.

"Who wants boring old toast," thought Flossie.

She decided to make her own special drink which always took a lot of preparation. It started with Ribena, then fresh orange juice, then some lemonade, four ice cubes and this particular Saturday she decided to look in the food cupboard and see what else she could put in.

She saw some Hundreds and Thousands, those

little chocolate bits you put on cakes, so she sprinkled them over. Then she put in a spoonful of honey and then a handful of almond slices. Honey and nuts were supposed to be very good for you, so Flossie had read somewhere. She tried to stir it all together, but there was such a gooey mess in the glass that she could hardly put her spoon in it. She took one sip, and it tasted yucky.

"Now what am I going to do with it?" thought Flossie.

She knew it would make a mess in the waste bin if she tried to throw it out, so she got out her best felt pens and paper and wrote out a little notice: "Keep Off. Preshus. Flossie's Speshul Drink. Do Not Touch."

She put the glass, with the notice, on a shelf in the fridge.

"Fergus is such a greedy pig," thought Flossie. "He's always taking my things. He's bound to see this notice and he'll drink it all up, being a greedy pig."

Flossie then made herself a simple Ribena drink and settled down to watch television. She always liked the Saturday morning programmes, such as "Sesame Street" or "Tiswas".

Saturday was also the day she got her pocket money from her father, but she had already had that two days ago—and spent it. She now needed the money desperately for something, but she couldn't quite remember what it was.

"Sweets or chips?" thought Flossie. "Must be one of them." Those were the things she usually needed desperately in life. Now she had a whole weekend ahead, without either sweets or chips. It wasn't fair.

Her father came downstairs next, drank a quick cup of coffee, put on his track suit and took Fido out for a jog.

Then her mother arrived, also wearing a track suit. She went into the garden, ran round the lawn ten times, then had two cups of coffee. Flossie could hear her mother counting as she was watching the television. Sometimes her mother would be thinking about other things and would run round the garden twice, then have ten cups of coffee.

Her mother then took off her track suit, went into the hall and started shouting for Bella and Fergus to wake up. She always had to do a lot of shouting, every Saturday morning, in fact every morning of the week, to waken them up. Lazy pigs, thought Flossie, as well as greedy pigs.

Fergus had to get up as he was playing in a football match and Bella had to get up as she had her Saturday job to do. That was the most unfair thing of all. Bella got pounds and pounds and pounds every Saturday for her job, and even more pounds in tips. Just because she was eighteen. The whole world was unfair.

"Why can't nine-year-olds have jobs?" thought Flossie.

Fergus eventually appeared and Flossie could hear him crashing around in the kitchen as he made his breakfast.

"Ugh," shouted Fergus. "I've been poisoned! Ugh! Mum, Mum, come quick!"

Flossie and her mother ran into the kitchen to see what was wrong. Fergus was holding the glass of Flossie's special drink.

"It's horrible," said Fergus. "I'll probably have to go to hospital, oh, oh . . ."

"You've been drinking *my* drink," said Flossie.

"Well, I'm not drinking it any more. Not now. I don't want *your* germs."

Miss Button had been doing a lesson at school only the other day on germs. Flossie was a bit hazy on the details, but she knew that germs were horrid things and you mustn't pass them on.

"Fergus, you shouldn't have touched that drink," said Mother, picking up the notice which Flossie had written. "You know it didn't belong to you. Look at this notice. Well you'll just have to finish it now . . ."

Flossie went back to watching television, smiling to herself.

Her mother had already shouted for Bella several times. Now she went to the bottom of the stairs and started yelling that she was going to be late for her job. But there was no reply. So Mother went upstairs.

"Poor old Bella," said her mother, returning after a while to the living room and going to the telephone. "She's got flu. I'll have to cancel her job. I do hope they can get somebody. I've given her an aspirin and now she's gone to sleep. I hope she'll be better by tomorrow."

Mother phoned the restaurant where Bella worked every Saturday, then she told Flossie to be as quiet as a mouse all morning, just to give Bella a chance to sleep properly.

"I think I'll go out on my roller boots," said Flossie, "when this programme's finished. Then I'll stay out till lunch. O.K.?"

When the programme was over, Flossie went very quietly up the stairs to Bella's room.

Her mother had left Bella's door slightly ajar, so that she could hear Bella if she woke up and wanted anything.

Flossie put her head round the door and peeped in. It was hard to see where Bella was. She had given up sleeping on a proper bed a long time ago and now just slept on a mattress on the floor.

"Wish I could sleep on the floor," thought Flossie. "But I'm not allowed. It's not fair."

There were so many cushions and pillows all over the floor, and bundles and piles of clothes, and models and busts, that the room could be full of sleeping people, Flossie thought.

Flossie eventually managed to make out the bundle that was Bella. She had a quick peep and could see that Bella really was fast asleep.

She stepped carefully over the bundles and took Bella's fur coat from the coat stand. She carried it down the stairs. Luckily, Fido was out walking with her father, otherwise he might have barked or made a noise and ruined everything.

Flossie went out of the front door, stood on the steps, then very gently she put on the special fur coat, the one which was so rich and thick and luxurious. As she did up the buttons, she closed her eyes and wished very, very hard that she could be eighteen, just like Bella, old enough to have a Saturday job of her own.

When she opened her eyes, she found that she had become Floz, eighteen years old, doubling her age in the twinkling of an eye. The magic, if that was what it was, had worked once again.

In the street, the milkman had just got out of his van and was coming to the front door with the Teacakes' milk and orange juice. He stopped suddenly and nearly dropped the whole lot. He could have sworn he had seen a plump little girl of about

11

nine coming out of the house.

Where had she gone to? Perhaps he should get new spectacles.

Floz ran down the street and into the main road. She knew exactly where Bella worked every Saturday morning as she had been there several times with her father, for special treats of course. It was a hamburger restaurant, Flossie's favourite place in all the world.

"Bella's ill, so she's sent me along," said Floz to the manager.

"What a relief," said the manager. "I've been trying all morning to get someone, ever since her mother rang. Here, put on this apron."

Floz hadn't thought about that. If she took her fur coat off, she didn't know what might happen. Probably she would turn straight back into nine-year-old Flossie, then she would never be allowed to be a waitress and eat chips all day and get lots of money. Floz stood biting her lip, just as she used to do when she was nine.

"No, I tell you what," said the manager, turning round again, "you'd better sit at the cash desk till the cashier turns up. Everyone's late today."

Floz sat down at the little cash desk near the front door where it was quite cold. A fur coat was obviously quite useful. The only problem, thought Floz, was going to be the adding up. Miss Button had not yet done all the multiplication tables. Floz could only do her seven times table, and even then she made mistakes.

Floz looked at the cash till very carefully. There was a low humming noise. She was worried that it might be alive and was scared to touch anything in case it would bite her.

She could see lots of knobs and buttons and switches so she touched one, ever so gently. A little drawer popped out so quickly it hit her in the stomach.

"Good job I've got on my special fur coat," thought Floz.

She couldn't put the drawer back, though she knew there must be a special button somewhere which made it go in. She pressed one switch down, and a light started flashing, so she pressed it up again. She tried another knob which looked very important and a hand shot out, just missing her face. On the hand were printed the words "Thank you. Come again."

"Do you do take-aways?" said a lady coming into the restaurant and going across to Floz's desk.

"No, I don't do that till I'm in the Third Year Juniors," said Floz. "But I'm very good at my seven times table. Would you like to test me? Don't ask me seven times nine, though. That's a hard one. And I'm not so good on six times nine either . . ."

"What a ridiculous restaurant," said the lady. "I'm certainly not buying anything."

"I don't care," said Floz, putting out her tongue behind the lady's back.

Most customers were having only coffees so far and the bills were not very hard to add up. All the same, Floz just looked at them quickly, thought of a number, and said it straight out.

"That will be ten pounds," said Floz to two fat ladies.

"That's funny," said one of the ladies. "I added it up and it only came to three pounds. All we had was two coffees and four cream cakes . . ."

"Four cream cakes," said Floz. "You greedy things. No wonder you're so fat."

"I don't come here to be insulted," said one of the ladies.

"Where do you go?" said Floz.

"I want to speak to the manager," said the other lady.

"He's in hospital," said Floz. "Got taken ill suddenly. I'm in charge today. O.K., the bill is only one pound."

"Oh, that's good," said one of the ladies.

"Yes," said Floz. "And don't forget the tip."

She then told a party of children, aged about nine years old, that their ice creams were all free today, but they could pay her a big tip, if they liked.

"Thank you very much," said the children. "We're definitely coming here again." And they all went out smiling.

Floz could see the manager coming towards her and she worried for a moment that he was coming to tell her off.

"I like to see children smiling," he said. "You're obviously doing well. The cashier has now turned up, so I want you to go and help with the chips. It's getting near lunch so there'll be a rush soon."

All Floz had to do in the kitchen was take a big wire basket of chips from a deep sort of frying pan, shake the chips, then empty them into cardboard packets. It was the sort of restaurant where you could eat the chips at the table or take them away.

Floz ate six whole packets of chips, all on her own, and began to feel rather sick.

Very soon, she also began to find it terribly hot working in the kitchen, especially wearing her big fur coat.

The chef in charge, who could see how hot she was, came across and told her to take the coat off.

"I can't," said Floz.

"Is it your religion, then?"

"No, it's my mum," said Floz. "She says I've not to take my coat off."

"O.K. then, you'd better go and help on the ice creams and milk shakes."

It was perfect timing. Floz was becoming rather tired of chips and felt like moving on to something else.

There were six milk shake machines, for coffee, strawberry, lemon, orange, raspberry and chocolate.

It wasn't long before Floz added a seventh—chip milk shakes. She had put some chips in the pockets of her fur coat, in case she got hungry later, so naturally she tried dropping a few in the milk shake machine, just to see how it tasted.

"What was that milk shake?" asked one of the waitresses.

"Eh, one of my specials," said Floz. "They haven't gone to hospital, have they? Wasn't my fault. It's this stupid machine . . ."

"No, they want two more. Just the same . . ."

The manager was again very pleased with Floz. So she started experimenting with other mixtures. They were all a great success, especially the honey and nuts milk shake, the treacle milk shake, even the marmalade milk shake.

Her only failure was with her first fried egg milk shake. It was sent straight back. So she mixed it up again, this time adding HP tomato ketchup, telling the waitress it was the latest savoury milk shake. It was this time pronounced delicious. The manager was delighted. He'd never sold so many milk shakes in a morning before.

He then asked her if she would take over as

waitress as the restaurant was becoming very full. He gave her an apron and she put it on over her fur coat. It did look a bit funny, but the manager was now too busy to worry about such things.

"I'm obviously his most popular worker," thought Floz. "He can't possibly be cross with me."

Floz was given four tables in a corner to look after and a little pad and pencil to write down the orders. At long last. It was really what Floz had always wanted to do. When she'd been little, about nine years old, she'd played at being a waitress for hours and hours with her friend Sarah.

"What do you want?" she said to the first table, licking her pencil.

"We haven't decided yet," said the man.

"Well, hurry yourself up," said Floz. "I haven't got all day."

"Is everything on?"

"Is everything on what?" Floz thought he was perhaps making some remark about her wearing her apron over her fur coat. Then she realized he was referring to the menu.

"Yes, but I wouldn't have the chips," said Floz. "They're yucky. I made them hours ago. They just keep them heated up. Some of them are yesterday's."

"I see," said the man, looking carefully at Floz, rather alarmed by the sight of her. Then he studied his menu.

"I'll have the avocado to start with," he said.

"S'off," said Floz. She had started to write it down, then she scribbled it out.

"But you said everything was on. I just feel like an avocado."

"Well you look like one," said Floz. "Ha ha ha. That got you."

"Why is it off?" said the man, beginning to sound rather cross.

"'Cos I can't spell it," said Floz. She didn't even know what avocado was, anyway. "Soup, you can have soup, or salad. Easy words like that. They're all on today."

"All right then," said the man, "we'll have two soups, two salads and then four hamburgers and chips."

"What about the tip," said Floz. "You pay the tip first."

"What on earth are you talking about? I've never heard anything like it in my life."

"It's a new rule," said Floz. She then leaned over to whisper in the man's ear, which wasn't a very wise thing to do, as she still had bits of chips and remains of some strange milk shakes on her chin which landed on the man's smart suit.

"*You* don't have to pay anything," whispered Floz. "Everything is free today. Just don't tell anybody. All right? They'll all want free lunches."

"Thanks," said the man. "Are you new here?"

"Why?" replied Floz.

The man was looking at her carefully and Floz was beginning to wonder if he thought she wasn't a proper waitress. She knew she looked grown up enough, but had she perhaps been a bit messy and a bit cheeky?

But the man said nothing more, obviously pleased that he wouldn't be charged. Floz decided not to charge several people after that, if she liked them. It made her work so much easier. It meant she had fewer bills to write out. And she did get more money in tips. Very soon, however, she began to feel tired, running backwards and forwards carrying plates of food. Some people were very bad-tempered and shouted at her when she took a long time serving, but Floz usually got her own back.

As she was passing a lady who had been horrid to her, Floz deliberately let drop a little bit of mustard from a dirty plate. Luckily, the lady didn't realize what had happened, because she was wearing a big hat with flowers on. One of the flowers noticed, though. It changed colour, from green to yellow.

Then another lady annoyed Floz by constantly changing her order, after Floz had laboriously written it down.

"What a slow and stupid girl you are," said the lady.

Floz was trying to do joined-up writing, which she couldn't manage very well.

Floz noticed that the lady had taken off her shoes under the table and was sitting for comfort in her stockings.

When the customer changed her order yet again, Floz bent down to pick up a spoon which she pretended had fallen on the floor. As she did so, she poured some HP sauce into one of the lady's shoes. That would teach her a lesson, thought Floz.

Floz came back from the kitchen with the lady's order to find that sitting at one of her tables was her father.

Outside, she could see Fido tied up, waiting patiently. She gave him a wave, without thinking, and instantly Fido saw her and started wagging his tail and jumping up and down. Floz decided she had better hide.

"What about that man over there?" said the manager. "Hurry up. You're not tiring, are you?"

Floz was forced to go over to serve her father, trying to walk backwards, which meant bumping into several tables, but her father didn't seem to realize who she was.

"I just want a coffee, Miss," said her father. "If that's all right. I'm going home for lunch."

"And what about the dog?" said Floz.

"How terribly observant of you," said Father, turning and looking out of the window. "You are clever to have noticed."

"Yes, I am," said Floz. "*And* I can do joined-up writing."

Floz went to fetch the coffee and at the same time

she brought back a double "Yum Yum, Tum Tum Cheeseburger", the speciality of the House, a stupid name, thought Floz, but they tasted delicious. Floz had had four that morning. She had filled this one extra specially full of pickles and dressing.

"This is for Fido," she said, handing it to her father. "Special offer, today only. You either get a fancy paper hat, or a free burger."

"And you know his name!" exclaimed Father.

"I know everything," said Floz. "Thank you and have a good day."

Floz went back to the kitchen with a pile of dirty dishes which she had cleared away from her other tables. This was the bit about being a waitress she was beginning not to like. It was so messy, gathering them all up, and so heavy having to carry them.

She suddenly looked at her fur coat. Despite wearing an apron over it, she'd picked up bits of food when she'd been carrying the dirty dishes to the kitchen.

"My beautiful fur coat," said Floz. "What a mess." She went to the toilets and ran some water, hoping to wash off the marks. She was in such a hurry to get it off that she had undone one, two and then three

buttons, all in a great rush, without even thinking.

She felt her tummy go strange. She looked at the mirror and it seemed to be getting higher, as if it was rising up the wall. Just in time, she fastened the top button up again, very securely, and rushed back into the restaurant.

She looked at the clock on the wall and realized it was almost 1.30.

"Got to go now," she said to one of the other waitresses, handing over her apron.

Floz was almost home before she realized she had forgotten to collect her wages.

She felt she had worked very hard all morning, even if she had lost them some customers and perhaps ruined several machines and upset a few digestions.

"I should have stayed for my money," she thought.

Then she felt in the deep pockets of her fur coat. Of course, she still had her tips. She counted out almost three pounds. Not bad, for a morning's work.

Floz managed to get into her house and was able to creep up the stairs without anyone noticing.

Bella's door was ajar and she could see that Bella was still asleep. She took off the fur coat and hung it carefully on the coat stand.

"Bella is so much better," said her mother as Flossie came into the kitchen and sat down at the table. "She's slept all morning."

"Hmm," said Flossie.

"But she's not quite strong enough to come down for lunch. As you've been so good this morning, Flossie, making no noise in the house, you can have Bella's chips."

"I'm not hungry, Mum," said Flossie.

"What?" said her mother, looking alarmed. "Don't say you're sickening for something as well."

"That's funny," said Father. "I think Fido isn't feeling so well either. He's gone straight to sleep in the hall."

"He hasn't been eating anything this morning, has he?" asked Mother.

Father shook his head.

Flossie knew it was a fib, but *she* wasn't going to say anything.

4

Flossie Goes for a Drive

The Teacakes were coming down the motorway after spending a holiday with their grandmother in Scotland. No, they were not walking down the motorway. The Teacakes might do some silly things, now and again, but they don't walk on motorways. They were in their family car. Father was driving.

"Let's stop at the next service station," said Flossie, who was sitting in the back seat, jammed between her big brother Fergus and her big sister Bella. "Dad, Dad, Dad. You promised you would."

"Oh, shut up, Flossie," said Bella.

"Why should I?" said Flossie. "It's not closing time."

Bella deliberately pushed Flossie into the middle of the seat. At the same time Fergus, who was trying to read, pushed Flossie from the other direction.

They were always pushing her around, in every way, so Flossie thought.

"I want some chips," said Flossie. "And a milk shake. This next motorway café will have them. I know that."

"No, dear," said her mother. "I've got the picnic. We're going to have some lovely cheese and egg pie and brown bread and some nice salad. . . ."

"Ugh, horrible," said Flossie. "Well, I'm not having any of that rubbish."

Mr and Mrs Teacake hated motorway cafés. They always brought their own food with them and when it was time to stop and have a rest, they drove off the motorway and into the country and had a picnic in a field. Even when it was the middle of winter. Even when it was pouring with rain. That's what Flossie called being *really* stupid.

So Flossie sat in the car, all on her own, while they had their picnic.

She could see them sheltering beside a tree, all of them wearing their raincoats. She knew they were talking about her and smiling, looking in her direction. She didn't care.

She found two Mars Bars in a side pocket of the

car, both a bit soggy and pale-looking, but she scoffed them. They probably belonged to Fergus. She didn't care.

"Broom, Broom," said Flossie, sitting behind the steering wheel, pretending to drive. "Zoom, Zoom."

It was one of her life's ambitions to be able to drive. One of her many life's ambitions.

Flossie could just see herself in her *own* little car, a very fast sports car, or perhaps a Rolls Royce, zooming down the motorway, going from café to café. She would be completely in control, of her movements and of her life and of her food. No one bossing her around.

"Oh, if only I could drive," said Flossie. "I would zoom off this minute and leave them all behind, sitting looking stupid in that stupid field, having their stupid picnic . . ."

"Come on, Dad," said Flossie. "Go a bit faster."

They were now back in the car, heading for home.

"Look, it says on the thing that the car can do a hundred and twenty miles an hour," said Flossie.

"So why aren't you doing it? Come on. Don't be so mean. Just do a hundred miles. That's not much."

"Don't be so silly, Flossie," said Bella. "You don't understand anything."

"It's the law, Flossie," said Mother. "You are only allowed to do seventy miles an hour."

"Well, when I learn to drive, I'll do a million miles an hour. You wait and see."

"When you're eighteen like Bella," said Mother, "then you can drive."

"I want to be eighteen *now*," said Flossie. "It's not fair."

"You will be soon enough," said Mother. "You don't realize how lucky you are. It will all happen far too quickly."

When they were just an hour from home, Father decided he was feeling tired and fed up with all the road works. He told Bella she could take over.

Flossie could hardly bear it. She closed her eyes and muttered to herself as Father drove off the motorway on to another road, an A road. He stopped and put L plates at the front and back of the car and let Bella take the driving seat.

Bella had been learning to drive for a few months

now. She had occasional driving lessons but it was mostly her father teaching her, especially when they were on holidays.

Flossie did know a bit about driving a car. She had twice been allowed to sit on her father's knee and had even changed gears, when they were on a farm track, near their grandmother's cottage. In her mind, she already knew *everything* about driving.

"Go a bit faster, Bella," said Flossie. "You're useless. Change gear now. God, I could drive better than this."

Flossie felt it had been one of the worst car journeys she'd ever been on. No chips at motorway cafés and now she had to sit and put up with Bella doing something she so passionately wanted to do. "Oh God, it's just not fair," said Flossie.

"Don't say God, dear," said her mother, absent-mindedly.

Next day, when Flossie had just come back from school, the phone rang. Flossie rushed to answer it. Bella and Fergus were not home yet, being at Big School.

"I hope it's one of my friends," thought Flossie. When Bella was at home she was always on the phone for hours and none of Flossie's friends could ever get through.

"Hello," said Flossie. She was really supposed to give the phone number, but that was stupid. Everyone knew her voice. All her friends did anyway, and that was all that mattered.

"Miss Teacake?" said a man's voice.

"Ye-es," said Flossie. After all, she was Miss Teacake. It could of course be one of her own school friends being silly.

"This is the Acme School of Motoring here. I'm afraid we'll have to cancel your lesson booked for tomorrow."

"Ye-es," said Flossie, putting on her most grown-up voice.

"But we have a new instructor, who has just started, who could take you today. That at least would give you one lesson this week. Are you free?"

"No, I'm nine," said Flossie.

"What?" said the man, sounding very puzzled.

"Sorry," said Flossie. "I mean I'm ninety per cent sure I can make it."

Miss Button had started percentages only that day at school. Flossie had got top marks.

"I'll just look in my diary," said Flossie, rustling an old newspaper. "Yes, I can come right now."

"Good. Thank you, Miss Teacake."

Flossie ran up the stairs and straight into Bella's bedroom. She had already crossed her fingers, hoping that it would work.

"It *must* work," said Flossie to herself.

All she had to do was put on the fur coat and wish, very very hard. She couldn't think of a more important wish she could ever wish for. Driving a car, a real one, on her very own.

She closed her eyes, sank deep into the fur coat, wished very hard, and fastened all three buttons. When she opened her eyes, she had become eighteen once again, tall and thin, very much like Bella, so she thought, only much nicer.

It took Floz only ten minutes to walk round to the driving school which was in the middle of the High Street.

She'd never been in it before, though she had

passed it many times. It always looked so important and busy, with cars waiting outside, and people bustling in and out.

Inside, it was much smaller than she had imagined, little more than a hole in the corner of another shop. The new driving instructor was waiting for her. He had a moustache and was carrying a clip board.

"Miss Teacake," he said. "Ah good, your car is over there."

He pointed to it, obviously meaning Floz to get in first, so she did. She opened the rear door and sat down in the middle of the back seat, where she usually sat.

"It's lovely to have room for a change," she said. "Fergus and Bella are so fat they usually take all the space."

"Is this some sort of joke?" said the Instructor.

"Sorry," said Floz, jumping out again, realizing her mistake. "I was just testing the back seats. Very comfy. Yes, very nice. Now I'll try out the front seat . . ."

The Instructor got in the car beside her and looked at his clip board carefully.

"I see you've had three lessons so far."

"Have I?" said Floz, examining the dials and instruments at the front of the car.

It wasn't at all like her father's car. She knew what everything meant in his car, because her father had told her so many times. But she wasn't worried. She had always known it was easy to drive a car.

"Actually, I'm rather a brilliant driver."

"That's good," said the Instructor, putting the ignition key in. "Perhaps, then, you could be kind enough to show me how to start the car . . ."

Floz pressed the first switch she could see, and the windscreen wipers started furiously going backwards and forwards. So she switched them off.

"Just testing," said Floz.

She touched another switch, and the indicator lights came on. She tried several others, but nothing much seemed to happen, though there were some strange clicking noises. The Instructor sat patiently, tapping his fingers on his clip board. Floz looked at him and smiled sweetly.

"You're new here, are you?" she said to him, very politely, putting on her charming voice.

"You are the one who seems to be new, Miss Teacake."

"Horrible," she said. The Instructor tapped his fingers even faster.

Floz touched another switch and this time it came away in her hand, so she passed it over to the Instructor. He gave a loud yell, screaming that he had been burned. What a funny instructor, thought Floz.

"That's the cigarette lighter, you idiot," he shouted.

"Oh, sorry," said Floz. "I thought perhaps you would like a cigarette. To calm your nerves. You do look a bit nervous."

"No wonder," said the Instructor. "Look, that's the key there. Let's have no more of this nonsense."

Floz turned the key and the car jumped into life, which was rather a shock to Floz. She had not realized that you could feel the engine vibrating through the driving wheel. Sitting in the back you hardly notice these things. Floz decided it felt very exciting. She couldn't wait to get out of town and zoom up the motorway. There was only one problem—what did she do next? Steering would be very easy. Any fool could do that. It was just this stupid car needed starting.

"Highway Code," said the Instructor.

"What?" said Floz. "No, it's a fur coat." The Instructor did have a funny way of talking, breathing heavily through his nose.

"Look in your mirror," he said, rather bad-temperedly.

Floz put her hand in her pocket. Being eighteen, she naturally carried around with her some of her make-up. She took out a little hand mirror. Yes, her mascara had run slightly, and her lipstick was rather smudged. Floz carefully attended to her face, then put the mirror away.

The Instructor gave a very heavy sigh. It was his first day at the Acme Driving School, but already that afternoon he had had problems with two teenage drivers, neither of whom seemed to understand anything he told them.

"Look in your *driving* mirror," he shouted. "Before you start, always look at your behind."

"Don't be rude," said Floz.

He gave a rather wintery smile. He should perhaps have chosen his words more carefully.

"All right, then," he said. "Let's take this very slowly. Now, press the clutch down." He pointed to the left hand side pedal, explaining what it was for, just in case this learner driver had already forgotten everything she had been taught.

Floz tried, but nothing happened. She was wearing stiletto heels, being eighteen years old, and one of them had got stuck in the floor of the car.

"Silly me," she said, "I'd forgotten I had these shoes on."

"I'll change the gear for you," said the Instructor. "Just let the clutch out slowly. Slowly! Don't jerk it. Now at the same time, press the accelerator."

Eventually, with the Instructor's assistance, Floz managed to drive the car away from the kerb and into the line of traffic.

Once she got going, Floz soon decided it was really quite easy. When it came to steering, as she expected, that was very simple, so she thought.

"Right, turn left here," said the Instructor.

Floz thought about it, looked down the side street, which she knew quite well, a very boring little street, always jammed with parked cars. Why should she. She wanted to drive properly. She pressed the accelerator harder.

"What are you doing?" he said. "I said go left."

"Hold on," said Floz. "Don't be so bossy. I'm not nine years old you know. I'll do what I like."

Floz drove slightly faster, going through a traffic light at orange, just missing colliding with a large red double-decker bus.

"Stop," said the Instructor. "I want you to stop here."

"Oh, these boring shoes," said Floz. "I'm going to drive in my bare feet." She kicked off her stiletto heels.

Floz felt so much freer without her shoes on and it encouraged her to drive even faster. She took one corner at such speed that the Instructor, who had expected her to slow down and obey the road signs, was thrown against the side of the car, giving his head a dreadful bang.

"Sorry about that," said Floz.

There was silence from the Instructor. Floz gave him a quick glance, swerving as she did so. Perhaps he had dazed himself, she thought. She leaned over, stretching in her seat belt, and listened to his chest.

"Still breathing," she said. "You'll be all right."

HAMPSTEAD
VIA CAMDEN
24
IT'S SAFER BY RAIL
ACME DRIVING SCHOOL

She started humming to herself, expecting the Instructor to tell her to stop and concentrate on her driving, but there was not a sound from him.

"Fallen asleep, have you," said Floz. "Well, you just lie back and enjoy yourself."

Floz was soon doing forty miles an hour. She had decided to carry straight on. She didn't want to do any of that going slowly round boring old corners and definitely none of that dreary reversing which she knew Bella did all the time.

She remembered how to get on to the motorway, having done it so many times with her father. She wanted to get there and open the window, to let the wind blow her long pink hair, just as she had seen in the films on television.

Once Floz was on the motorway, she quickly zoomed up to seventy miles an hour. She thought perhaps she would not break the speed limit, not this first time. She looked at the Instructor, to see if he was watching her. His eyes were tightly closed.

Floz felt marvellous, roaring along the motorway. As usual, there were several road works in progress, but that did not stop Floz. She ignored all the signs and deliberately went on the side of the road that was being mended. She could see that there were no cars there at all.

It was a bit bumpy when she got to the part being repaired, but all the workmen very kindly jumped quickly out of the way.

"Thank you very much," yelled Floz. "Very good of you."

Floz zoomed straight ahead, giving them her film star's wave.

She thought about going into a motorway café, as she was beginning to feel a bit hungry and thirsty, with all the speed and excitement, but if she stopped the car, how would she ever get it started again? So on she went, zoom, zoom, broom, broom, roaring through the countryside.

It all seemed so simple to Floz. Going fast on the motorway meant there was no need to change gear, no need to brake. She just pressed the accelerator to go fast or slow, and turned the wheel.

"I don't know why people make such a fuss about driving," said Floz. "It's easy peasy."

SITE OFFICE
L
ACME DRIVING
SCHOOL
L
RANGE ROVER

Very soon, she realized it must be time to return. Her mother would wonder where she was and the driving school would be wanting the car for the next lesson. The Instructor still appeared to be asleep.

At the next junction, she slowed down slightly and turned off into the left-hand lane. She went up on to the motorway bridge, then down the other side and back on to the motorway again.

Floz was now heading for home, without having had to stop or reverse. She felt very pleased with herself. Quite a few cars got into the side of the road as she went past them.

"They must be admiring my driving," thought Floz.

She got back into town quite quickly. By now her driving had improved and she was able to slow down much better and managed to pull up safely outside the driving school.

There was a car in front which helped to slow her down. It was only a little bump at the front. No one would ever notice, thought Floz.

The Instructor woke up almost as soon as Floz

stopped the car. He gave his head a shake and looked round, rather bemused. He rubbed his eyes, felt his head, stared out of the window and then stared at Floz. He saw that they were now back home, outside the driving school, which was where they should be, and that the car was in neutral, also as it should be. And the hand-brake was on. Floz beamed, feeling very pleased with herself. She had at least remembered what to do when you parked a car.

"Jolly well done," said the Instructor, getting out. "I'm only sorry I won't be able to take you next week. You're a rather quick learner . . ."

Floz walked slowly home, still going "broom broom, zoom zoom," under her breath, and sometimes even over her breath. She went up to Bella's bedroom and carefully unbuttoned the fur coat and hung it in its usual place.

"Oh, Bella," said Flossie over tea. "Your driving lesson is off tomorrow. They rang up this afternoon to cancel it."

"Thanks, Flossie," said Bella, being quite human to Flossie for once. "It's a relief, really. I've got a busy week and it's such a strain, having a driving lesson. You'll realize that one day, Flossie. It's not as easy as it looks."

"I'm sure you're right," said Flossie, very demurely.

5

Flossie Goes to Big School

There was always a lot of noise and commotion every Monday morning in the Teacake household. It often sounded as if a football match was going on inside. Or perhaps the Teacakes were getting ready to go off to battle, shouting and yelling and shrieking to frighten their enemies. It was only the Teacake children getting ready for school, and Mr and Mrs Teacake preparing to go to work.

Mr Teacake was the only one who ever got upset by the noise. He maintained that everyone in the town could hear them shouting. The rest of the family didn't seem to care, or didn't seem to notice, or were too busy shouting to hear him.

"How can I hear to read my newspaper," he said, "with all this noise going on?"

"You don't have to *hear* to read," said Flossie.

"You just have to see to read."

"Don't be so clever, Flossie," said Bella.

"Oh, shut up, you," said Flossie.

"No, you shut up," said Bella.

"Why should I?" said Flossie. "I'm not a door."

Most families make a *bit* of noise on Monday mornings, but perhaps the Teacakes made slightly more than most.

Monday mornings always came as something of a surprise to Mrs Teacake. Getting to Sunday evening should have been a clue, but somehow she always forgot.

The first Monday morning problem was money. They never seemed to have enough change in the house. That was what usually started off all the noise.

All three children, Bella, Fergus and Flossie, needed to be given their dinner money for the week. And all three children insisted that *they* had to have the exact change.

Bella and Fergus, both being at Big School, which was a few miles away, also needed money for their bus fares. Very often they also had to have extra money for school funds, for clubs, for outings.

So every Monday morning, poor Mrs Teacake scurried around the house looking for change. She searched in old handbags, in old purses, in trouser pockets, in jacket pockets, under beds, on top of shelves, down the sides of sofas, in tins, mugs, cups, and even in teapots. Mrs Teacake did leave money in the most surprising places. It wasn't that Mrs Teacake was absent-minded. She was just slightly forgetful, having much more important things on her mind.

At last, she had gathered together enough pennies and other coins to keep them all happy, with the help of Flossie's piggy bank and Fergus's secret horde of birthday money which he kept locked in a tin box.

"Who's pinched my maths book?" said Fergus. "Flossie, where is it?"

"I haven't seen any of your stupid books," said Flossie. "So shut up, you."

"Oh, not that again," said Bella.

That was usually the second stage in the Monday morning noise. Once the change had been sorted out, then the Teacakes started losing things, or accusing people of taking their things, or hiding them, which of course was silly.

Why should Flossie, for example, want to take Fergus's maths book? Well, lots of reasons. Just to annoy him, that could be one reason. To get her own back, that might be another reason.

Mr Teacake turned out to have Fergus's maths book. It was underneath the newspaper he was reading, or trying to read, exactly where Fergus had left it. He had been doing some last minute homework while he'd been eating his breakfast.

Flossie was very lucky, so her mother always said. She could walk to school in only a few minutes, which meant she could leave later, and not have to worry about bus fares or waiting in queues.

Flossie was at Primary School, so she had no homework to do and no books to carry to school, unlike Bella and Fergus. They were both at Big School and often left home in the morning loaded down like camels.

But Flossie did not consider herself lucky. Certainly not. "*They* are the lucky ones," so Flossie thought.

Flossie was particularly jealous of Bella who was

in the sixth form and could do anything in this whole world she wanted to do. It wasn't fair.

First of all, Bella went to school as if she was dressed to go to a party. At Bella's Big School, you could wear anything you liked, once you were in the sixth form. Bella always wore make-up and long jangly ear-rings and any clothes she fancied.

Flossie had seen Bella going to school in her grandfather's raincoat, another time in a sack, or what looked like a sack, and another time in an Indian sari and another time with just a blanket wrapped round her. On one occasion, Flossie had seen Bella go to school in bare feet.

"Oh, it must be lovely to go to school like that," thought Flossie.

Flossie always had to wear sensible shoes, because her mother insisted, and she couldn't wear jeans, as the headmistress did not approve of jeans, until you were in the fourth year of the Juniors. Flossie was only in the second year.

At Flossie's school, you were not allowed to wear make-up or any sort of jewellery, not even ear-rings. Miss Button was against ear-rings, for boys and girls. At Bella's school, so Bella had told Flossie, even the boys could wear ear-rings. It simply wasn't fair.

Then at Flossie's school you always had to go out in the playground at every break, no matter what the weather was like. This really upset Flossie. She wanted to be able to stay inside school if she wanted, just to mess around, sit talking to her friends or even do some reading. It was stupid, so stupid, she thought, always being forced to go out into the playground.

Bella never seemed to go in the playground at all. Most play times, Bella stayed inside the school with her friends. She could even make coffee or tea and have biscuits in their own special room.

Flossie's class had two naughty boys in it, Billy and Tommy, and whenever they were naughty, Miss either made them all stay in late after school or took a star off every person in the class.

"That's the most stupid thing of all," so Flossie thought. "Why should I be made to pay for Billy and Tommy being naughty?

"If only I was at Big School like Bella. I've never heard of *anyone* at Bella's school being punished or told off. It's just not fair."

Next day happened to be Tuesday, which even Mrs Teacake realized came after Monday. Tuesday was never a worry to her. The worst of the week's noise and commotion was over by then.

On this particular Tuesday, she had forgotten at first that Flossie had the day off. It was a one-day holiday at Flossie's school. She had the note somewhere from the Headmistress, telling her what the reason was, but she couldn't quite find it, even looking in both teapots.

"Hooray," said Flossie. "A whole day off from that stupid school."

She told her mother that she planned to play in the street most of the day with her friends, although when she saw Bella getting ready for Big School after breakfast, wearing this time what looked like silk pyjamas, she wished she was going with her.

"We've got a sixth form open day today, Mum," Flossie heard Bella tell her mother. "It's for other sixth forms to come and look at our classes."

Bella often went to other schools for lessons, and other sixth formers came to her school. Bella just seemed to wander around all day as she felt like it.

GUARD DOGS
KEEP OUT

She had no set hours. Sometimes she left at nine in the morning, and was home by ten o'clock.

"Imagine being able just to come and go when you want to," thought Flossie. "That's what school *should* be like."

When Bella had left home, Flossie decided that after all she wouldn't play out with her friends. She listened carefully, just in case Bella came back for something, as she often did, then she went quietly up to Bella's room. The fur coat was still there, where Flossie had last left it.

"Oh, how I wish I was at Big School," said Flossie. She put on the fur coat, buttoned it up, and closed her eyes very tightly.

Once again, when she opened her eyes she found she had turned into Floz, eighteen years old. She now looked for all the world the very model of a modern sixth former.

Floz knew where Bella's school was, as she had been there several times, to school plays and jumble sales, but she had never been inside it on a normal school day.

It looked so much bigger than she remembered it. As for all the children, many of them were enormous. Some of them seemed like giants, compared with the children in Primary School.

Floz watched one or two of the really big boys arrive driving their own motor cars. Two of the big girls even came on motorbikes. At Primary Schools, children never drive themselves to school, but then life at Primary School, thought Floz, can be rather boring by comparison.

Floz saw one boy coming through the gates who was wearing a moustache. Or could it be a joke moustache? Bella, after all, often dressed for school as if she was going to a fancy dress ball.

She thought about hiding behind a pillar and then jumping out and tweaking the boy's moustache, but she thought better of it. She was still a bit scared, by the size of the building and by all the large children.

"Perhaps he's a teacher, not a boy," thought Floz. "At this Big School, it's hard to tell the difference between children and teachers. Perhaps he is the Headmaster!"

Floz smiled. She knew that at Big School you could be anything.

Floz stood for a while in the entrance hall. There were hundreds of children going up and down the stairs and along all the corridors.

In a Primary School, you stay in your classroom almost all day long, with the same teacher. In a Secondary School, every lesson has a different teacher in a different room, often in a different part of the school.

"It must be very confusing when you're new," thought Floz.

As she was wondering which way to go, she saw that someone was waving at her. It was Martin, Bella's friend.

"Looking for the sixth form common room?" said Martin.

Floz didn't know what she was looking for really, but she nodded her head.

Martin took her into a huge room full of battered chairs and couches. She could see lots of big boys and girls, all just sitting around. Some seemed to be sleeping, some reading newspapers, some listening to records. Some even seemed to be smoking. Nobody was bossing them around.

"I wish my school was like this," said Floz.

"What's your school like, then?" asked Martin.

"Well, it's sort of different," said Floz. "You would lose three house points if you put your feet on a table like that boy over there."

Martin laughed. He liked Floz's silly jokes, or what he thought were her silly jokes. Then he took a piece of paper out of his pocket and examined it quickly.

"What's that," said Floz. "A weather forecast?"

It did look to Floz like one of those weather charts you see on television, but a very big one, perhaps for the whole world.

"It's my timetable," said Martin. "I've got to go now. Physics."

"Fizzy what?" said Floz, never having heard of such a thing before. "Can I have a drink as well?"

Martin showed Floz where the coffee machine was, then he rushed out of the common room.

Floz stretched out on a couch with her coffee, turning over the pages of a pop music newspaper, looking at all the photographs.

"Ah, this is the life," thought Floz. "Every school should be like this. No work and all play."

"You're a prefect, aren't you?" said a man with a beard, putting his head round the common-room door, looking straight at Floz.

Floz wasn't sure what a prefect was. Perhaps it was like Physics. So she nodded her head.

"Right, look after class 1B till break."

He then disappeared so Floz went out into the corridor. There were signs on the wall and eventually she found a door marked 1B. She looked through the glass window in the door and saw about thirty children, aged about eleven, sitting at their desks, all writing in their books.

Floz walked into the room and went to the teacher's desk. At first, all the children carried on working away, but slowly they stopped writing and sat watching Floz, waiting for her to speak.

"Miss, what shall we do now?" said one boy at the front. He looked a bit cheeky, almost like Billy or Tommy.

Floz was not quite sure what they should do now, but she had always wanted to be a teacher, or a nurse, or a model, or a pop star, or a gymnast, or a ballet dancer, or a waitress. But being a teacher had been her *first* ambition.

"What's five and seven?" said Floz. The boy looked puzzled.

"Hurry up, boy," said Floz, putting on her sternest voice. "*You* won't be getting a star today, I can see that."

They all looked puzzled.

"What's seven nines?" said Floz, turning to another boy. "No, that's too hard," Floz added quickly. She had remembered that she herself was not quite sure of seven nines.

"O.K., who wants to do sticking and cutting? We'll do that instead."

"It's supposed to be Algebra, Miss," said a boy.

"Who is Algebra?" said Floz, thinking it must be the name of a boy. "Right, Algebra can do the sticking and cutting then. You can be milk monitor."

They all started laughing, so Floz smiled, thinking she had made a good joke.

"Should we get on with our own work now?" asked a girl at the front.

"That's a good idea," said Floz. She was beginning to wonder what she could do with the class.

Floz walked round the room as they all worked,

trying to look serious, which she soon found very boring. There were one or two naughty boys who started talking, and then banging their books, and she was worried that the bossy-looking man with the beard might come back.

A loud bell suddenly went off, which gave Floz quite a fright, and she thought for a moment it was one of the naughty boys playing tricks. The whole class jumped up and rushed out of the room. Floz was quite glad to realize that the lesson was now over.

"Perhaps it's not such fun after all being a teacher," thought Floz.

Floz went back into the sixth form common room, just as Bella was coming out, holding a pile of books. Bella looked very cool in her silk pyjamas. Floz was beginning to feel very hot, buttoned up in her fur coat.

"Hi," said Bella. "There's a cloakroom over there where you can leave your coat. I'll take it if you want."

"Eh, no thanks," said Floz, realizing just in time.

Bella seemed to give her a very hard stare, so Floz thought.

"It's English now," said Bella. "Are you coming?"

That sounded interesting to Floz. At least she knew what English was. She had been one of Miss Button's best spellers.

There were only about twelve people in the English class, all very grown-up looking, sitting around comfortably. The teacher looked very nice as well, wearing jeans and plimsolls.

He was talking about some play by somebody called Shakespeare, someone Floz had never heard of. It was like a foreign language.

Floz tried to leave after fifteen minutes, but the teacher gave her such a look she decided to sit down for a little longer. Now and again the teacher asked questions, on what certain bits meant. Luckily, he didn't ask Floz. Bella seemed to know quite a lot of the answers.

Floz had not realized there could be any boring bits at Big School. At Primary School, Miss Button hardly ever talked for more than ten minutes about anything. And if you got bored, you could just get up and walk round the classroom, go to another table, join another group, do some sticking or painting.

The teacher went to the blackboard and began to write out some lines of poetry, none of which made sense to Floz.

"They don't even rhyme," thought Floz. "Stupid old Shakespeare, or Spearshaker, or Cheesecake, or whatever he's called."

While the teacher's back was turned, Floz jumped up and went out of the classroom door. She had decided it was about time she moved on.

On her way through the corridors, she heard some teachers, or perhaps they were prefects, or perfects, telling off smaller children. That looked good fun.

"Stop chewing, boy," Floz shouted, creeping up behind one boy of about twelve who practically jumped out of his skin. "Give me the packet."

Floz took the packet from the boy and put all the chewing gum in her mouth.

"Walk on the *left* hand side of the corridor!" Floz shouted at one quite big girl of about sixteen years old. The girl stopped, then walked on.

"Right," said Floz. "Bring me a hundred lines by four o'clock."

Floz wasn't quite sure what sort of lines that meant, but she had heard someone else shout it. She hoped it wasn't lines written by that boring poet Shakingbum.

She saw someone running ahead so she ran even faster in order to catch up with him.

"No running in the corridor!" Floz bellowed, putting on her fiercest voice. The person turned round. He was wearing a beard and looked very much like the man she had seen earlier.

"School play," said Floz. "I'm just practising for the school play. Sorry . . ."

Floz ran off quickly down a corridor till she came to a door. She opened it quickly and went straight in, closing it behind her.

Floz looked around, her eyes opening wider and wider. She was in the most marvellous gym, equipped with all the latest apparatus. At her Primary School, they didn't have a proper gym. They just used the school hall, the one in which they had morning assembly and where they also had school dinners. When it was gym time, they simply pulled a few ropes and mats out of a cupboard. It had always seemed so unfair.

There were lots of girls, most of them slightly smaller than Floz, climbing up the wall bars, jumping over wooden horses, swinging from parallel bars, bouncing on a trampoline, swinging from rope ladders which hung from the ceiling.

There didn't seem to be a teacher in sight, so Floz decided to show them a few tricks. She'd always loved doing gym, even when she was small and fat and wore spectacles. Now she was tall and lean and lithe. She would show them a thing or two or even three.

Floz bounded across the floor, turning cart-wheels, then leapt straight over the vaulting horse. She was fortunate that her fur coat didn't get stuck on the top of the wooden horse, but she went so high that she seemed to be flying, her fur coat billowing behind her.

"Come here, girl," said a stern voice from the door. Floz looked round and saw a woman in a short skirt with very strong legs. Floz stood for a moment, wondering what to do. It was like being back at Primary School, having teachers being so bossy.

Then she walked slowly over to the teacher.

"That was very good, girl," said the teacher. "Now, I want you to do that again. This time, *without* your coat."

The teacher held out her hand, waiting for Flossie to hand it over. Floz started to obey, not wanting this lady to shout at her any more, forgetting for a moment that she was after all a grown-up girl of eighteen.

All the other girls had stopped practising and were standing watching Floz. They'd all been very impressed by her gymnastic ability.

Floz undid the bottom button of her fur coat, then the next, but as she touched the top button, the one she was now beginning to believe must be a magic button, her body gave a little shake.

"Sorry, Miss, I've got to go," said Floz. With that, she dashed past the teacher, out of the door, down the corridor.

Floz didn't stop running. She found the front entrance to the school and tore out of it, still running. She flew like the wind, all the way home.

She remembered that her mother had promised her fish fingers and chips for lunch, if she was a

22
10

good girl. She had been a terribly good girl. She had occupied herself all morning.

As Bella was still at school when Floz returned home, it was easy for her to take the special fur coat upstairs and hang it carefully on the coat stand.

"Big School is more fun than Primary School," said Flossie to her mother as they both sat at the kitchen table, eating their lunch together. "Isn't it, Mum?"

"It is in some ways, dear," said Mother.

"But you have to do some boring things, don't you, Mum?" said Flossie.

"You might think so now, dear," said Mother. "At your age, dear."

"And you have to listen to some very boring people," said Flossie.

"How do you know, dear?" said Mother.

"I just do," said Flossie.

"The most important thing about Big School," said Mother, "is that you have to do a great deal of work."

"Yes, dear," said Flossie, to her mother. "Perhaps I'll stay at Primary School for just a little bit longer . . ."

6

Flossie Goes to the Disco

Flossie carefully put the living-room chairs against the wall and picked up the best rug and rolled it into a ball. She always needed lots of space for dancing.

She thought about moving all the big cushions into another room but decided they would be handy in the middle of the floor. Good for falling on, especially if some of her hand-stands and cart-wheels didn't work out quite right.

Flossie had been watching "Top of the Pops" recently on TV and had picked up a few ideas for some new routines. She always called her dances "routines", just like the professionals. She looked round for somewhere safe to put her specs. Usually, she had her eyes closed when she danced, so that was one reason for not needing her spectacles. She also put the lights off, or at least made them dim, so that was another reason for not needing them.

"Horrid things," said Flossie, doing a few stretches and bendings in front of the mirror. "I'm glad to get them off."

Flossie was in her best leotard, the yellow one, which she used for gym club at school. She did have a black leotard, which she used for ballet classes, but she considered she looked better in the yellow. It made her look thinner, so Flossie thought.

Over the top of her leotard she was wearing a sequined little number which her mother had made for her. She always called her dancing clothes "numbers". Just like the professionals.

"Or do you call the routines numbers?" Flossie wondered. "And are the numbers called routines? Hmm. It's all a bit confusing, being a professional dancer."

The sequined top had originally belonged to Bella who had bought it for 10p from a jumble sale, where she got all her clothes. Bella had never worn it, so Mother had kindly altered it for Flossie. Flossie loved it. She wanted to wear *all* Bella's clothes, all the time.

Flossie had tied up her hair into what she thought was a punk style. This had taken a lot of doing as the two elastic bands had twice broken and hurt her fingers, snapping at the vital moment.

"Oh, if only I could wear make-up," said Flossie.

She worried that everybody could see she was just wearing an old leotard and a cut-up top and her lipstick had been put on with a felt pen. It wasn't fair.

"When the lights go off," thought Flossie, "I can imagine that I'm dancing with John Revolting, or whatever his silly name is."

Flossie was at last ready for the dancing to begin. All she was waiting for next was her partner to arrive.

"Come on then, I'm ready," shouted Flossie, tossing her hair, but not too violently, just in case the elastic bands went twang and catapulted her head across the room.

"Hurry up," shouted Flossie. "I'm waiting."

As Flossie shouted, Bella popped her head into the living room. She laughed out loud when she saw Flossie in front of the mirror, practising steps.

"You look ridiculous, Flossie," said Bella. "And

who said you could wear that top? I want it back."

"One word," said Flossie. This was her latest smart remark.

"I want it back," said Bella.

"One word," repeated Flossie.

"Please," said Bella, bad-temperedly.

At that moment, Mother came into the room. She told Bella off for being horrid to Flossie, so that was nice for Flossie. Mother said that of course Bella didn't want the top back. Bella had never ever worn it.

"O.K., she can keep it then," said Bella. "I'll probably be quite late, Mum. Are you listening? I think I'll go to the disco. A *real* disco. 'Bye . . ."

"Have a nice time," said Mother.

Flossie looked in the mirror and put her tongue out at Bella, then she put on a pop record, very loudly.

"I'm still waiting," shouted Flossie once again.

Mother couldn't dance, couldn't sing, and was tone deaf. She could recognize only two tunes. One of them was *God Save the Queen* and the other wasn't *God Save the Queen*. She could never remember what the other was.

Mother disliked all music, especially pop music, and hated the fact that both Bella and Fergus had their transistors on all the time, even when they were doing their homework—most of all when they were doing their homework. Flossie didn't have a transistor. She had been given a cheap one last Christmas, but the batteries had gone. How could she buy new batteries on 25p pocket money a week? It wasn't fair.

"Oh, do hurry up," yelled Flossie.

Fido suddenly bounded into the room, almost knocking Flossie over. He was very excited and obviously expected that he was going to be Flossie's dancing partner.

When Flossie was *very* hard up, and had absolutely no one else to dance with, then she sometimes did jump round the room with Fido. He was very keen, but sometimes he would decide to roll over on his back, which was a bit inconvenient, if he was your dancing partner. It could also be very dangerous, if the dance happened to be taking place in the dark, as it usually was, when Flossie was in charge.

"Right," said Father, bursting into the room. "I'm ready at last."

Flossie had had to wait all this time because her father had been finishing his quiet sherry. He always had one when he came home from work, while he read the evening newspaper, and before he had his dinner. Flossie often wondered what a noisy sherry would taste like or sound like. Probably like Fergus. He made the most awful noise when he was eating.

"On one condition, though, Flossie," said Father, going to the record player and taking off her pop record. "Yes, you agree?"

"O.K., if you must. Boring old Beatles."

Father did love dancing and was quite good at it, considering he was an old man of forty years of age. It was just that he didn't like modern pop music, the stuff Flossie watched on television, especially that new group Flossie talked about with her friends at school. Some of her friends had never even heard of the Beatles.

Flossie put the lights off, leaving one little red lamp glowing in the corner.

She had tried several times in the past to switch the lights off and on while dancing, which was very awkward, dancing and doing the lights at the same time. She had been told by Bella that you had *flashing* lights at real discos, though that might just have been a fib, to make her jealous.

Father had been furious. He said the lights would fuse. Flossie had to stop it at once and never do it again. Otherwise, he wouldn't dance with her again. So Flossie had agreed.

The little red lamp in the corner was Flossie's own idea. There had been a red bulb left over from her last birthday party, on Hallowe'en, when her mother had disguised the living room as a witches' cave.

Flossie was very proud of the red lamp. She felt it gave the room a feeling of mystery and romance, making it all exciting. She could almost believe it was the real thing.

They danced for about ten minutes, then Father had to have a rest. He said his legs were tired and his back was stiff.

"After only ten minutes," thought Flossie. "What kind of dancing is this." But she didn't say anything.

Father was teaching Flossie to jive. She wasn't quite sure what jiving meant, but it was very complicated and when she did manage to do all the right turns, as Father twisted her round him, crossing arms, going round the back, and lots of other fancy twirls, it felt really rather good.

"I used to be a champion jiver," said Father, "when I was young." Flossie was quite proud. It was much better anyway than dancing on your own, which was what Flossie usually did.

They danced for another ten minutes, then Father said he was exhausted. He would have to have a rest, and anyway his dinner was nearly ready.

The record player was turned off, as Mother didn't like music on in the house, not when she was having her evening meal.

Flossie was left alone, looking at herself in the mirror.

"If only I had a *pink* leotard," thought Flossie, "that would be much better."

The more she looked at herself the more she decided that yellow was really a horrid colour, almost like a school uniform.

"Now what am I going to do?"

She knew there was nothing on TV. She was fed up doing drawing and sticking. That was just for Infants. She was too tired to practise her piano. Anyway, Mother had said she wanted no more noisy music.

Flossie was all dressed up but with nowhere to go.

Flossie went slowly upstairs to her bedroom. She hadn't really meant to go into Bella's room. She just found her steps going that way. Then her steps took her to the special fur coat.

She was wishing so hard, twirling around inside the fur coat, that when she had buttoned the top button she had done it once again. Flossie was now Floz, a beautiful, thin, lovely, no-spectacles, no-fat girl of eighteen.

Some old people might not have thought she was exactly beautiful, as underneath her fur coat she was dressed for a disco in the most weird clothes, all satins and sequins. But Floz thought she looked really great. Her hair was bright green this time. It stuck out in the air like a starfish.

Floz left the house without anyone seeing her,

though silly old Fido came barking towards her in the hall, hoping for a dance, a dog's excuse-me dance, but Floz gave him a quick pat, then quietly let herself out of the front door.

She knew the name of the disco where Bella went, The Pink Elephant, but wasn't quite sure where it was. She'd heard Bella say it was next to Marks & Spencer, which seemed a funny place.

"Imagine doing disco among the knickers and the frozen chickens," thought Floz.

There was a little side door beside Marks & Spencer which she had never seen before and a notice saying "Entrance—£1." She hadn't thought about that. She put her hand in her fur coat pocket, but she had no money. How was she going to get in?

"This way, Miss," said a rather fierce man as the door suddenly opened. He had been watching Floz through a peep-hole in the door.

Floz decided it must be because she looked so terrific, in her brilliant disco dancing clothes. Or perhaps he thought she was famous, the world's eighteen-year-old champion disco go-go girl.

"Girls free before ten o'clock," he growled, holding out his hand for her fur coat.

Floz declined his offer. She wasn't going to let that fur coat out of her sight, ever. Who knows what might happen? It would be so embarrassing if she suddenly turned back into her old self again, right in the middle of a number, or even a routine.

However, she unbuttoned her coat slightly, to reveal her amazing Technicolor dream coat outfit. Nothing awful happened. She didn't become nine again. Anybody looking at her could clearly see she was at least eighteen, if not twenty-eight.

It took Floz some time to work out what was going on. She thought for a moment she was upside down, or perhaps the world was upside down. All the dancers were on a glass floor which had lights underneath and dazzling mirrors all around. Bodies seemed to be flashing and twirling and turning everywhere, in the sky and in the ground.

It had never been like this, not when she used to dance with her father. The noise was frighteningly loud. It was shaking not just her ears but her whole body. She felt as if she would be blown apart by the noise.

Very slowly, Floz became more used to the sound and the sights. She realized that all the dancers were dancing individually, not holding each other, the way she expected. They were gyrating on their own, mostly on the same spot. They seemed to be in a dream, their eyes closed, concentrating very hard.

Someone waved from the far corner and she realized it was Martin, Bella's boyfriend. They were all sitting together at a table, drinking Coca Cola, so she went across to join them.

"Hi," said Martin. "Haven't seen you for a long time."

"You should get new specs, then," said Floz.

"I used to wear specs when I was nine," said Martin. "And a brace on my teeth. It was hell and I hated it. Now look at me."

Martin gave a big smile, opening his eyes and holding his mouth open.

"Horrible," said Bella. "You'll frighten the animals."

"Shall we boogie?" said Martin to Floz. She wasn't quite sure what boogie meant, but she nodded her head.

"Groovy," said Floz. She didn't quite know what groovy meant, but her father often said it.

Martin took her on to the special dancing floor which worried Floz at first, in case she might fall as it looked so slippery. It wasn't at all like dancing on carpets. It took her a little while to get used to it.

She looked around for the DJ's turntable and noticed he was in a kind of box on a platform at one end, raised up, with lots of flashing lights. Then she heard his voice announce the next groovy, boogie number. He must be Wild Willie, the resident DJ. He seemed to be working much harder than they did on "Top of the Pops".

Martin didn't actually do much dancing, which was a disappointment for Floz. He made some rude remarks about the DJ, though Floz could hardly hear him for all the noise. Martin just seemed to stand there, rocking slightly on one foot, clicking his fingers.

"Don't you know the steps?" said Floz.

"I'm trying to give them up," said Martin.

Most people seemed to be dancing in much the same way as Martin and very soon Floz decided it was rather boring. She hadn't expected real disco dancing to be so un-exciting. She quite enjoyed standing on the spot, wiggling her hips, but really, once you'd done that for ten minutes, it was a bit monotonous. She could do all that at home.

Floz and Martin sat down when the record had finished and Floz was quite relieved.

Just as the next record was about to begin, the DJ came out of his little box and on to the glass floor, still holding his microphone.

"It's Rock 'n' Roll Revival time, boys and girls, guys and dolls," he shouted through the microphone. "And this lovely couple here is going to demonstrate how to do it. Come on now, a big hand for Sharon and Darren.

"When they've finished, I want you *all* to have a go, guys and dolls. Don't forget now, there's a big prize for the lucky winner. Let's go!"

The two dancers took the floor on their own while everyone else crowded round to watch them. Floz at once recognized the steps. It was just like jiving. She had done the steps herself, oh years ago, with her father.

When they had finished, the DJ called for volunteers. No one came forward at first, so he went round, pushing people on to the floor. He came to Floz almost at once.

"I've been watching you, baby," the DJ said to Floz. "You're really super, something else, groovy, baby. You *must* have a go."

Once Floz got on the floor, Bella and Martin and all their friends also decided to have a go.

Very few people could do the steps properly. If you've always danced on your own, it is hard to dance with a partner. People were falling over their own feet, or falling over their partners' feet. The DJ went round, making the worst dancers leave the floor.

Bella and Martin were among the first to be asked to leave, but the DJ was nice to them. He made them sit at the side and showed them how to move their hands in what he called a hand jive.

Floz thought it looked very babyish, patting your hands in time to the music, one hand on top of the other, like One Potato, Two Potato. But Floz was too busy dancing to take much notice...

Very soon, Floz was one of the few dancers left on

the floor. Darren, the demonstration dancer, came over to partner her, while his partner Sharon danced with another boy. That left just two couples on the floor.

The music was changed to "Can't Buy Me Love" which was Floz's favourite Beatles tune.

She felt excited as she jived around, going through all the old steps she had learned with her father, plus some that Darren led her into, plus some they made up as they went along.

She seemed to be floating in the clouds and for much of the time she really was in the air as Darren threw her over his shoulders, under his legs, round his back. Her fur coat billowed out like a cloak, making their steps even more dramatic, hanging on her shoulders by one button.

There was tremendous applause when finally they finished, most of all from Bella and Martin.

The DJ came forward to present Floz with a brand new LP, made by that new group, who had become Number One in the charts only that day. He took Floz up on to a little stage and everyone crowded round, clapping and cheering. Some even shouted "Speech, Speech!"

"A big hand for our best dancer ever," said the DJ, taking Floz's hand. "And an even bigger hand for her fur coat! Wasn't that just a fantastic outfit, guys and dolls!"

Everyone clapped once more and Floz let the DJ slip off her fur coat. She was feeling incredibly hot, with all that energetic dancing, and was very pleased not to have it on for a change.

"And now," continued the DJ, "as it's just before midnight, we're going to have a slow, smoochy number . . ."

The whole disco suddenly seemed to grow very quiet. Nobody was listening to the DJ or looking at him. They were all staring at Floz. Something amazing was happening before their eyes. Floz's body was getting smaller. The tall, lean, thin, lithe and beautiful girl was slowly starting to disappear. In her place, or so it appeared, a little girl was emerging.

"Quick, give me that coat," screamed Floz, grabbing it from the DJ's hands. She had realized at last what was happening to her.

"I've got to go. Sorry, it's past my bedtime . . ."

She threw the fur coat over her shoulders and quickly buttoned the top button. She was imme-

diately eighteen again, much to the surprise of the people near the front of the little stage. Those at the back blinked their eyes. They hadn't understood what had happened to Floz and were now beginning to doubt if anything had happened at all, or that they had just imagined it.

Floz then grabbed the new LP, which she had won for her brilliant dancing, jumped down from the stage, pushed her way through the crowd, and raced for the door.

"An encore, please," the crowd roared after her. "Just one more dance . . ."

But Floz was in the street. She stopped only to button up her fur coat completely, just in case, then she ran as fast as she could for home, the cheers of the dancers still ringing in her ears.

Floz let herself in and crept upstairs, put the fur coat back safely in Bella's room, and then fell into bed, absolutely exhausted. She hadn't even bothered to look in the mirror to see if she was Flossie. As she snuggled down into her bed, she wondered if her ears would ever be the same again.

Flossie was sound asleep when at two minutes past midnight, Father came in to tuck her up. He was a little later than usual tonight. With his supper, he had had three quiet glasses of wine, which always made him rather late.

"Good night, Flossie," he said, bending over and giving her a kiss. "Sleep well."

He noticed on the floor beside Flossie's bed a brand new LP record.

He picked it up and looked at it.

"All right then, Floss," he whispered, "next week we'll dance to some modern music. I promise."

In her sleep, Flossie seemed to shake her head and give a little smile, then she put her hands over her ears and turned over.

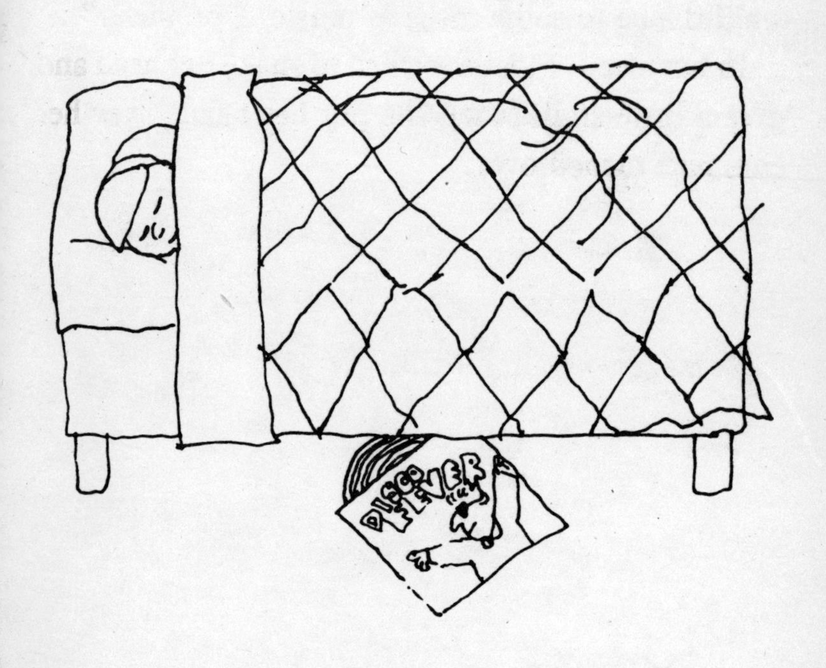
DISCO
FEVER

Hunter Davies

Flossie Teacake's Fur Coat
Flossie Teacake – Again!

What Flossie wanted most in the world was to be a teenager like her sister Bella, to be tall and thin and wear make-up and jangling earrings and dye her hair pink.

Flossie, ten years old, tries on Bella's fur coat, and suddenly all her dreams begin to come true. A series of wonderful adventures for Flossie, exuberantly told and matched by Laurence Hutchins's lively illustrations.

The Fiend Next Door

SHEILA LAVELLE

Charlie Ellis lives next door to Angela Mitchell whom she once described in a class essay as 'My Best Fiend'. Living next to Angela is a mixed blessing. Angela has the most remarkable ideas and somehow Charlie always seems to get involved. The trouble is that Angela's plans have a horrible habit of going badly wrong and more often that not it seems to be Charlie who ends up getting the blame. It was, after all, Angela who borrowed the baby and pretended that she had kidnapped it but it was Charlie who got landed with looking after it – and trying to put it back. Also Angela is not above a little deviousness when it suits her. She certainly stopped at nothing to get her hands on the bag that Charlie had been given though, in the end, Charlie got her own back with vengeance.

Terrible though Angela can be, Charlie has to admit that life would be very dull without her around.

Also in Young Lions are *My Best Fiend* and *Trouble with the Fiend*.

Simon and the Witch

MARGARET STUART BARRY

Simon's friend the witch lives in a neat, semi-detached house with a television and a telephone, but she has never heard of Christmas or been to the seaside. However, she has a wand, which she loses, causing confusion at the local constabulary, and a mean-looking cat called George, who eats the furniture when she forgets to feed him. The witch shows Simon how to turn the school gardener into a frog, and she and her relations liven up a hallowe'en party to the delight of the children and the alarm of the local dignitaries. With a witch for a friend, Simon discovers, life is never dull.

Very highly recommended by ILEA's *Contact* magazine: '. . . who could resist such a lively character?'

You will find more adventures of Simon and the Witch in *The Return of the Witch*, *The Witch of Monopoly Manor* and *The Witch on Holiday*, all in Young Lions.

The King of the Copper Mountains

PAUL BIEGEL

For more than a thousand years King Mansolain has reigned over the Copper Mountains, but now he is old and tired. To keep his heart beating, he must hear exciting stories.

So one by one the animals of his Kingdom come to tell their tales – the fierce wolf, the chattering squirrel, and the three-headed dragon, breathing fire. The beetle sits close to the King's ear to tell his story while the other animals lie on his beard. Next comes the mighty lion and last of all, the dwarf. He prophesies that the old King *could* live a thousand more years, but only if the Wonder Doctor arrives in time . . .

For eight-year-olds and upwards.

My Best Fiend

SHEILA LAVELLE

'My best friend is called Angela Mitchell and she lives in the house next door.' There is nothing unusual about this opening description Charlie Ellis gives of her best friend, but the tales that follow reveal the very unusual scrapes these two friends seem to get into.

Pretty Angela's marvellous ideas usually lead to disaster. Like the time they got stuck on a single-track railway bridge over the River Thames with the rattle of train wheels getting closer and closer; and the time Angela accidentally caught an escaped circus lion in the back garden. But when Angela suggested burning down her dad's garage so that he could claim the insurance for a new one, Charlie really thought things had gone a bit too far. For somehow it's always plainer Charlie who ends up taking the blame, and the spelling mistake in her English essay really wasn't much of a mistake at all.

Private, Keep Out!

GWEN GRANT

I have written a book. It's all about the street we live on – me and our Mam and Dad, and our Pete and Tone, and Lucy, Rose and Joe. They're my brothers and sisters, worse luck.

I don't see why I should be nice to that stuck-up dancing teacher Miss Brown just because Pete's going to marry her, and how *can* you tell if angels are really men or women?

Growing up in a north-east Midlands colliery town just after the War, the narrator, youngest in a family of six, is never out of trouble. She is high-spirited, impulsive, stubborn and often exasperated by her parents and older brothers and sisters, but she will win the heart of every reader in her determined efforts to keep her end up.